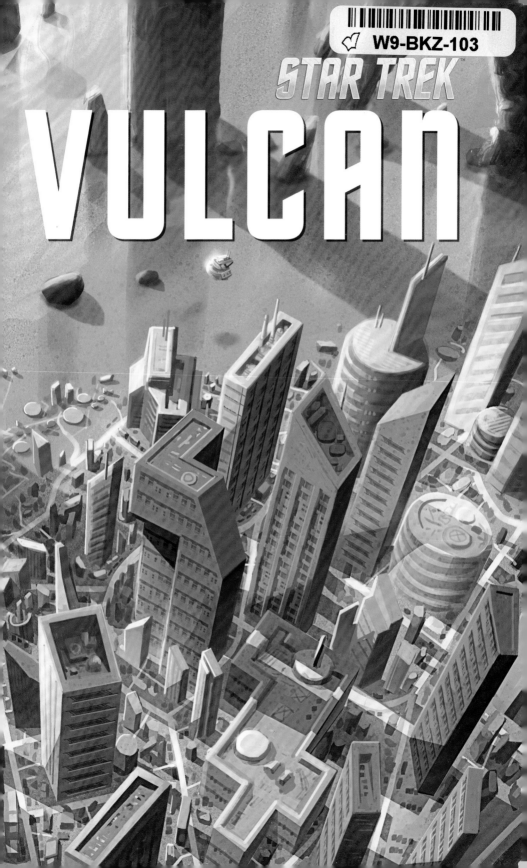

STAR TREK

# VULCAN

# STAR TREK

# VULCAN

## DAYTON WARD

ILLUSTRATIONS BY
### LIVIO RAMONDELLI
AND
### PETER MARKOWSKI

INSIGHT EDITIONS
San Rafael, California

# CONTENTS

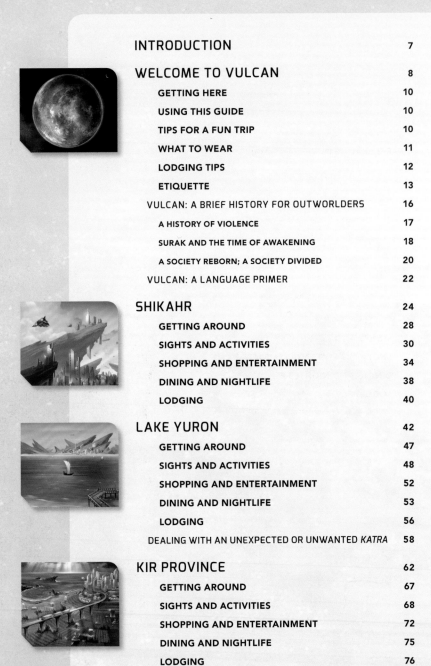

# INTRODUCTION

GREETINGS, TRAVELER, FROM THE PEOPLE OF THE PLANET VULCAN.

That you have chosen our world as a focal point of your examination of other cultures evokes satisfaction in our people. Over the course of the past century, Vulcans have learned to better appreciate the notion of visitors from other worlds experiencing our society firsthand. This is due in large part to our long association with humans of the planet Earth, who seem endlessly fascinated with anything and everything they encounter. While our relationship with humans has at times been trying—and mine in particular, given my dual Vulcan-human heritage—my people realized long ago that we can learn much by interacting with other species. With this in mind, we have increased our efforts to foster a welcoming atmosphere on our planet and to establish organizations with the primary goal of ensuring a memorable experience for all who visit our world.

Vulcan history is long and multifaceted, filled with successes and failures, triumph and tragedy. Once, we were all but consumed by emotions and violence, and it was the acceptance of logic and reason as our guiding principles that kept our civilization from annihilating itself. It has only been within the last few generations that the Vulcan people have allowed the full extent of our cultural heritage to become known to outworlders. Again, we have our friends from Earth to thank, for they are the ones who showed us how sharing our story also benefits us, as we too have learned from the sharing.

As a visitor to Vulcan, you will discover that we observe many customs and protocols. These practices have been described by some outworlders as rather ritualistic in many ways. Our adherence to these time-honored traditions, like almost every other aspect of our society, is rooted in logic, but there is more to our people than this dedication to reason, as visitors already familiar with our people know. If this is your first time visiting our world, we hope you will take the opportunity to not just travel to various points of interest, but also immerse yourself in our culture and discover all that we have to offer.

Live long and prosper,

Spock
Vulcan Ambassador to the Federation
July 2387
(Federation standard calendar)

# WELCOME TO VULCAN

*"Logic is the cement of our civilization, with which we ascend from chaos using reason as our guide."*
—T'Plana-Hath, matron of Vulcan philosophy

## GETTING HERE

Vulcan is located in the 40 Eridani A star system. The planet is open to visitors throughout its solar year, but outworlders are advised to be aware of the numerous celebrations and festivals that may complicate a recreational visit. While many of these events are open to non-Vulcans, be prepared for activities that are private or otherwise restricted to "locals only."

## USING THIS GUIDE

You'll note that many of the names for commercial establishments in this guide are rendered in Standard, or are named in accordance with the Federation's common language. In reality, most of these businesses carry some sort of Vulcan name. The merchants we contacted for this guide supplied appropriate translations or their own tourist-friendly alternatives to simplify locating them. Don't be surprised to see both "real" and "tourist" names on the front of most retail establishments. This will be true for all but a few historical sites, as you'll see throughout this guide. Thanks to the planet's real-time global positioning sensor network, it's all but impossible to get lost on Vulcan.

## TIPS FOR A FUN TRIP

- Travel overland whenever possible. Visitors have access to air vehicles at most tourist-friendly locations around the planet, and transporters are available, but don't cheat yourself out of the opportunity to observe Vulcan's wondrous terrain from ground level.
- There are a number of popular routes that use magnetic-rail trains to connect major population centers with landmarks and other points of interest. Personal desert flyers and other hovercraft are also available for rent or charter.
- Try to fit in an overnight camping trip at one of the numerous sites in or near Vulcan's Forge. Hiking trails with experienced guides will lead you to natural landmarks, ancient ruins, and eye-popping scenery.
- Remember that you're visiting a desert planet. Humanoids and similar life forms are strongly encouraged to drink sufficient daily quantities of water—or whatever nutrient equivalent is appropriate for your species.
- For those of you who breathe oxygen, remember that Vulcan's atmosphere is thinner than that of many worlds that are home to humanoid species. Also, the gravity here is higher. Depending on your physical condition and individual physiology, you may require an acclimation period before undertaking any strenuous activity.
- There's a distinct possibility that the planet might not exist in all realities, universes, and timelines. Check with your travel agent for details.

## WHAT TO WEAR

There's a reason they say, "hot as Vulcan." The planet's arid, desert climate means plenty of hot days and cool nights, so dress in one or two layers of light clothing made from natural fibers or synthetic substitutes that allow ventilation. Assuming you have appendages, long-sleeve shirts and pants are encouraged, particularly with cuffs you can close to prevent sand from finding its way inside your clothing. Robust footwear suitable for hiking is an absolute must. A light jacket is usually enough for most nighttime activities. During the day, species with sensitivity to light and heat are encouraged to supplement their wardrobe with protective eyewear as well as wide-brimmed headwear.

With respect to colors and styles, you can get away with pretty much anything in the larger cities, but more conservative dress is encouraged in the smaller provinces and especially in the various temples and historic or religious sites. When hiking in the desert, avoid bright primary colors, as they tend to attract predatory animals. Be especially aware of the *le-matya*, a large, wolflike beast possessing poisonous claws and uncanny speed.

##  LODGING TIPS

Guest lodging is plentiful in all of the larger population centers as well as the other regions that attract a large number of visitors. Major cities like ShiKahr and Vulcana Regar offer accommodations for numerous species from throughout the Federation, but don't expect such variety in smaller towns or outlying areas. "Be adaptable" should be your motto in these situations. Reservations are encouraged at any time, especially if you're planning a visit during a prominent event or celebration.

While hotels and other accommodations in the larger cities and prime tourist hot spots often feature diverse staffs with employees representing any number of races, this will rarely be the case in smaller towns and in the provinces. When arriving at your hotel, remember that Vulcans aren't rude or even brusque by nature—unlike, for example, the Tellarites, who long ago elevated arguing to an art form. Instead, Vulcans are simply straightforward in most interactions. Unless the hotel employs non-Vulcans, don't expect small talk or friendly chitchat while checking in or during your other dealings with members of the staff. In more remote locales, be prepared to observe Vulcan customs and traditions throughout your stay. For example, Vulcans are early risers, and meals at many hotels are served on a precise schedule. In fact, punctuality is the order of day in all things, so be late for breakfast at your peril!

## ETIQUETTE

Vulcans are a private, seemingly aloof people. Though they generally welcome outworlders, visitors should be mindful that they may encounter occasional reticence toward strangers, particularly from older members of the population and in those areas that are less traveled.

Though many Vulcan customs and traditions have become familiar to outsiders thanks to centuries of integration with other worlds, Vulcans prefer to keep certain things to themselves. Much has been written about the *pon farr*, for example, but it's still impolite to inquire about this challenging aspect of Vulcan biology, which occurs every seven years of adulthood and robs Vulcans of their emotional control. Few, if any, Vulcans are willing to openly discuss such matters, and almost never with outsiders.

When moving about in public areas, visitors are reminded to restrain themselves with respect to displays of emotion. No, the entire planet isn't a giant monastery, but those hoping for an experience similar to Carnival or Mardi Gras on Earth are encouraged to forego a trip to Vulcan and instead consider an extended stay on Risa or Wrigley's Pleasure Planet.

While it's true that representatives from numerous worlds live and work here, there are still areas where outworlders are not permitted. These areas are noted throughout this guide, and tourists are encouraged to familiarize themselves with local customs and protocols whenever they travel to a new location.

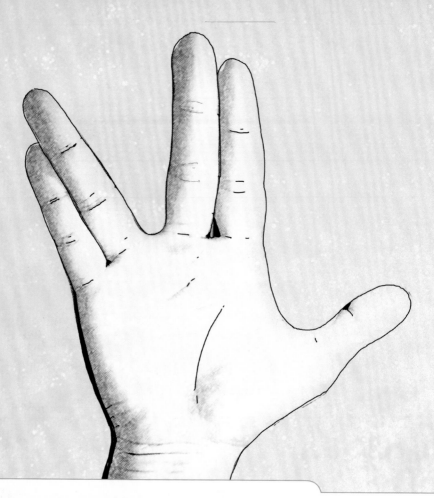

# DID YOU KNOW?
## SAYING "HELLO" AND "GOODBYE" ON VULCAN

Most Vulcans will acknowledge straightforward salutations such as *Greetings* or *Good day*, along with more casual forms of address like *Hello*. However, Vulcans tend toward formality and tradition when greeting or bidding farewell to one another.

Unlike other species, Vulcans do not shake hands or otherwise touch each other when offering a salutation. Physical contact between Vulcans is a very private, even intimate, act, and it is rare to see such displays in public. What you will see is the customary hand gesture, with the greeter offering the salutation *Sochya eh dif*, or "Peace and long life." The party receiving the greeting returns the hand gesture and replies, *Dif-tor heh smusma*, or "Live long and prosper."

Don't be afraid to greet and say goodbye to Vulcans in this manner. Even if you bungle it the first time, Vulcans will likely appreciate the effort and courtesy you're extending to them. Just be prepared to have any deficiency in your delivery corrected.

# VULCAN: A BRIEF HISTORY FOR OUTWORLDERS

A PLANET RICH IN HISTORY and culture and boasting a population of more than six billion, Vulcan stands apart from other Federation worlds as home to one of the most intriguing of all civilizations. The people of Vulcan thrive in a wondrous dichotomy between the ancient and the modern, the traditional and the progressive, the reserved and the chaotic. How is all of this possible from a society that prides itself on strict adherence to logic and conformity? The answer to that question is itself shrouded in layers of contradiction.

## A HISTORY OF VIOLENCE

Most outworlders know that Vulcans, despite their celebrated devotion to logic and strict emotional control, were once an aggressive, even barbaric people, embracing a warrior culture similar to that at the heart of the Klingon Empire. During the Age of Expansion, as it's now known, Vulcan clans combined their numbers, establishing permanent settlements in order to protect areas that offered food, water, and shelter from the planet's unforgiving environment. Most conflicts during this period were waged over control of such resources, and this innate societal aggression led to the Vulcan people being decimated by several civil wars. At one point, more than two thousand years ago, they found them-selves on the brink of annihilation.

## SURAK AND THE TIME OF AWAKENING ▶

As yet another war seemed inevitable, Surak, a Vulcan philosopher, renowned scientist, and outspoken pacifist, increased his efforts to end the protracted aggression and bloodshed. He enlisted emissaries from his growing legions of followers to carry forth his message of peace to the planet's various governments and military leaders.

Even in the face of repeated setbacks and the deaths of many of his most ardent supporters, Surak held true to his beliefs until he too died in battle. Despite this tragic loss, Surak's message of tolerance and inclusion—the celebration of *Kol-Ut-Shan* or "Infinite Diversity in Infinite Combinations" not just among the Vulcan people but indeed among the limitless varieties of peoples found throughout the universe—soon began to take hold. This turning point in history is known as the Time of Awakening. Because of his unwavering values and leadership, which allowed his people to master their emotions and accept reason and logic as a means of guiding them from the darkness of unremitting conflict, Surak remains the most respected of all Vulcans.

## DID YOU KNOW?
### THERE WERE VULCANS ON EARTH BEFORE OFFICIAL FIRST CONTACT.

According to the accepted story of the first contact between Vulcans and humans, the crew of a Vulcan spacecraft, while conducting a survey of the Sol system more than three centuries ago, detected a warp-powered vessel and traced its source to Earth. There, the Vulcan crew members first encountered humankind.

What many people don't know is that Vulcans had already visited Earth more than a century prior to this historic first meeting. After a small scout craft crashed in a remote area of North America in the mid-twentieth century, the two surviving crew members spent months living among humans and waiting for rescue. A recovery ship eventually arrived on Earth to take the two survivors home, but not before they had received an unprecedented opportunity to observe humanity at a time prior to many of the great social and technological achievements that would come to define it.

## A SOCIETY REBORN; A SOCIETY DIVIDED

While some might view them as an isolationist society, Vulcans in truth have long been prominent players in interstellar politics. Following the cessation of their numerous civil wars, the Vulcan people turned their formidable scientific and artistic abilities to the renewed development and expansion of their civilization.

This was not a universal societal goal, of course, and a portion of the population was not content to follow Surak's teachings. Not wishing to distance themselves from their emotions, tens of thousands of discontented Vulcans banded together. Knowing they would never be welcome on their home world, they marshaled the necessary resources to seek a new future among the stars. This monumental exodus came to be known as "the Sundering," a schism between two fundamental sects of the Vulcan people, which remains unhealed to this day. These dissenters eventually found their way to a pair of worlds in a distant region of space, and it was these two planets that would form the foundation of the Romulan Star Empire.

On Vulcan, progress proceeded apace under this new Age of Reformation. Though the effort took more than 1,500 years, the Vulcan people eventually returned to space and even discovered the ability to travel faster than light. A far-reaching space exploration initiative brought them into contact with numerous worlds and other civilizations, such as the Andorians, Tellarites, and the humans of Earth.

Not all of these encounters were pleasant, of course. For example, Vulcan's initial interactions with Andor were quite adversarial and included a series of confrontations along their shared territorial boundary. Even after formal hostilities ended and a truce was declared, elements of the Vulcan government, space service, and intelligence community continued to be suspicious of the Andorians. This eventually resulted in a rather embarrassing incident in the twenty-second century when Starfleet inadvertently discovered that the Vulcan government was covertly monitoring Andorian activity along their shared border.

This was but one of several incidents that led to resistance from a group of Vulcans known as the "Syrrannites." Named for the movement's founder, Syrran, this group carried out a prolonged protest against the Vulcan High Command, which they felt was moving away from Surak's philosophies and becoming increasingly militaristic. After a bombing at the Earth embassy on Vulcan was blamed on the Syrrannites, Starfleet officers assisted in the investigation and discovered leaders within High Command had orchestrated the attack. With Starfleet's help, the rebels ultimately succeeded in removing the corrupt leadership and installing a civilian government overseen by T'Pau, a prominent Syrrannite leader who would go on to become one of Vulcan's most renowned leaders.

In 2155, Vulcan entered into the Coalition of Planets, a formal alliance with Andor, Earth, and Tellar Prime. It was this collective that would eventually stand against the Romulan Star Empire. Following the bitter four-year conflict known as the Earth-Romulan War, the Coalition gave way to what we now know as the United Federation of Planets (UFP). Beginning in 2161 with just the original four signatory species, the Federation has since grown to include billions of beings representing more than 150 different worlds. Vulcan itself provides a key voice in interstellar relations and politics both within and beyond the Federation's borders.

# VULCAN: A LANGUAGE PRIMER

**IN AN AGE OF UNIVERSAL TRANSLATORS,** and with most UFP member worlds having adopted Federation Standard as the official spoken language, communicating with the locals has never been easier. On Vulcan, Standard is the common language in the public spaces of the major cities, though you may encounter occasional reticence or outright refusal by some locals to speak in anything other than their native dialect. A universal translator will see you through most of these situations, assuming the area you're visiting allows such modern technology. In places where universal translators are prohibited, try to travel with a tour guide—they should be able to help navigate the less friendly encounters. While we obviously can't include a comprehensive Vulcan language guide here, we can at least provide you with some of the most common terms and phrases you should know.

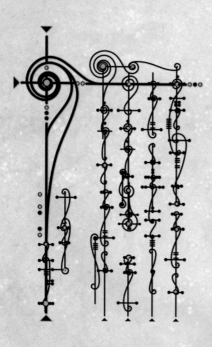

*Chaya t'not:*
**Thank you.**

*Nam-tor puyan-tvi-shal wilat:*
**Where is your restroom?**

*Nam-tor rom-yokul-mahr-kel wilat:*
**Where is a good restaurant?**

*Nam-tor wak ra:*
**What time is it?**

*Ni'droi'ik nar-tor:*
**I am sorry.**

*Sochya eh dif:*
**Peace and long life.**

*Dif-tor heh smusma:*
**Live long and prosper.**

Additionally, you will find that most Vulcans employ elements of their own language in everyday Standard speech. This can be for several reasons, such as a desire to observe tradition. You'll likely hear at least a few of these key terms during your visit:

*Ahn-woon:* The oldest of traditional Vulcan combat weapons, which resembles an Earth sling. In modern times, it is often used during various rituals and ceremonies.

*Fal-tor-pan*: Also called "the refusion." An ancient ritual used to reunite a Vulcan's *katra*—a Vulcan's living spirit—with their physical body. Do not try this at home.

*Kahs-wan*: A ten-day test of survival, courage, and maturity undertaken by Vulcan children and conducted in the unforgiving climate of Vulcan's Forge.

*Katra*: A "living spirit," or the essence of a Vulcan's intellect. When death is near, some Vulcans are able to transfer their *katra* into the mind of another living being.

*Kolinahr*: The purging of all emotions and the embracing of total, pure logic.

*Kol-Ut-Shan*: The Vulcan philosophy of "Infinite Diversity in Infinite Combinations."

*Koon-ut-kal-if-fee*: An ancient ritual that translates to "marriage or challenge." In the event that a female Vulcan does not wish to be married to the male partner arranged for her during childhood, she can choose a defender to challenge her betrothed. The actual challenge part of the ritual is known as the *kal-if-fee*, or "passion fight," during which a Vulcan can confront another to win the hand of a prospective wedding partner. Tourists are encouraged to avoid such ceremonies, as participants fight to the death, and spectators have been known to find themselves drawn into these skirmishes.

*Lirpa*: A traditional Vulcan combat weapon that consists of a staff with a fan-shaped blade at one end and a bludgeon at the other. Today, it is one of the weapons used during ceremonial proceedings such as the *kal-if-fee*. Nonlethal versions can be found in many gift shops.

*Pon farr*: The Vulcan "time of mating," which affects Vulcans approximately every seven years of their adult life. This aspect of the Vulcan reproductive process is dominated by a neuro-chemical imbalance that impedes logic and rational thought and is often likened to a period of "madness." Left untreated, the condition can prove fatal. As the imbalance worsens, the afflicted Vulcan will enter a state of *plak tow*, or "blood fever." While the condition can be treated through medita-tion, it can only be truly remedied by successful mating with a bonded partner or through a similarly intense emotional experience, such as undergoing the *kal-if-fee* combat ritual.

*Suus-mahna*: A defensive martial art. Unarmed combat experts often compare it to such Earth disciplines as aikido and jujitsu.

*T'hy'la*: A term of endearment, loosely translated as "friend," "brother," or "lover."

# SHIKAHR

LUCKY
LATINUM
LAGOON

# SHI

MULTI-
CULTURAL
MERCANTILE
DISTRICT

SHIKAHR
PINNACLE

VULCAN HIG

QUARK'S

SURAK

MEMORIAL GARDEN

T'PLANA-HATH
HISTORICAL MUSEUM

SUBSPACE

VULCAN
SCIENCE
ACADEMY

HALL OF VOICES

INTERPLANETAI

# HR

VULCAN
SPACE CENTRAL

SHIKAHRAOKE

...ND

THELIN'S
...RAL EXCHANGE
...RFORMING
...RTS CENTER

FIR'CREETA
SHIKAHR

...DRANN

T'VELA
SOCHYA

...FE PRESERVE

- ● SHOPPING & ENTERTAINMENT
- ★ DINING & NIGHTLIFE
- ▲ LODGING

**VULCAN'S CAPITAL CITY,** while not the largest in terms of geography, is still the busiest population center on the planet. A model of modern engineering and technical achievement, ShiKahr is also steeped in history. According to those few records that still survive as well as countless hours of archaeological research, the city is believed to be the focal point for nearly every major societal and cultural turning point in Vulcan civilization. Ancient buildings and monuments still bear the scars of numerous invasions that occurred long before the Time of Awakening, and stories of the heroic sacrifices made to preserve these timeless treasures are well chronicled in Vulcan literature as well as those historical accounts that still exist. These same ruins now stand side by side with contemporary, towering edifices that—much like the Vulcan people—continually reach for the skies and the stars beyond.

Museums and libraries abound in ShiKahr, showcasing the work of Vulcan artists in addition to those from other worlds. Thanks to ShiKahr's many embassies representing other Federation member worlds, the city has become a melting pot, boasting a richly diverse population. Much like Tokyo, San Francisco, or New York City on Earth, ShiKahr is an effervescent metropolis that never seems to rest, and visitors can find something of interest at any time of day or night.

##  GETTING AROUND

Public transportation is the norm in ShiKahr. Airborne vehicles as well as mass transit above and below ground connect each of the city's major sections and operate around the clock. Additional transportation options can take you from ShiKahr to every other major city or point of interest on the planet. You'll find that ShiKahr is a healthy city, where various forms of self-propelled transportation are promoted, particularly with regard to tourists.

## SHIKAHR: CRADLE OF INFINITE DIVERSITY IN INFINITE COMBINATIONS (IDIC)

It is said that the city of my birth is the epitome of Vulcan society. While I consider such observations to be reasonably accurate if somewhat simplified, I also believe that these descriptions fail to recognize one of the capital city's greatest strengths. ShiKahr is nothing less than a living, breathing example of what it means to embrace one of our guiding principles, "Infinite Diversity in Infinite Combinations."

Despite our well-earned reputation for observing tradition and our many formal, even ritualistic, procedures and protocols, my people welcome a vast tapestry of cultures. Since joining the Federation more than two centuries ago, Vulcan has played host to immigrants from numerous worlds, and several of our cities have grown to become thriving cosmopolitan centers, each showcasing a vibrant mixture of cultures. There is much to experience here, and I hope you find your visit worthwhile, enlightening, and memorable.

—Ambassador Spock, 2387

# 👁 SIGHTS AND ACTIVITIES

Due to the multicultural impact of Federation membership, ShiKahr can look and feel as much like a collection of smaller cities as it does a single thriving megalopolis. Ancient stone streets and buildings intermingle with state-of-the-art infrastructure and architecture. Nowhere is the Vulcan IDIC philosophy more evident than in ShiKahr, where you'll find no end of shops, restaurants, gardens, museums, and art galleries representing dozens of worlds.

## Cultural Exchange Performing Arts Center

The city's largest entertainment venue stands at the center of the Multicultural Mercantile District and plays host to a seemingly unending series of musical concerts, stage productions, athletic competitions, and even political rallies. Though Vulcan culture and performing arts are a cornerstone of the activities taking place here, the center's advertised goal is "to celebrate the arts in all their infinite forms." To that end, it hosts an eclectic range of programs. Musical and theater festivals dominate seasonal schedules, and the center is the anchor point for the annual ShiKahr Fringe Theatre Festival. Though the venue is quite popular for private gatherings, most events are open to the public. You probably won't get to crash a wedding, but as tourism has expanded here, Vulcans have increasingly welcomed visitors to participate in holiday observances and other celebrations that at one time would have been all but forbidden to outworlders. Be sure to take advantage of these opportunities if your trip coincides with such an occasion.

## ◀ Embassies

ShiKahr is home to more than 150 embassies of varying size and appointment, representing each of the Federation's member worlds, with most of them located at points along or near the perimeter of the Multicultural Mercantile District. More embassies are in the planning stage or in the first stages of construction, slated to host diplomats from new or more recent member planets. Most of the embassies have areas open to the public, and many even have their own small museums, art galleries, and other points of interest, each chronicling their respective world's relationship with Vulcan and the period leading up to the Federation's founding.

## Hall of Voices

Some of Vulcan's most celebrated philosophers, diplomats, and pundits have stood at the center of this hallowed chamber. Located in a subterranean amphitheater near the grounds of the Vulcan Science Academy, the Hall has borne witness to some of the greatest debates over centuries of Vulcan civilization. The sessions are open to all, and, in traditional fashion, speakers present their positions on their chosen topic and then invite discussion and rebuttal from other speakers as well as the audience. It was here that Vulcan officials debated joining Earth, Andor, Tellar Prime, and Alpha Centauri to form what would become the United Federation of Planets.

## ▲ Surak Memorial Garden

Reflecting pools and gardens are everywhere in ShiKahr, but none are as breathtaking as this one at the city's center, which stands in eternal tribute to Surak, considered by many to be the father of modern Vulcan civilization. The life-size bronze statue bearing his likeness stands before a stone representation of the Vulcan symbol for *Kol-Ut-Shan*, or "Infinite Diversity in Infinite Combinations." The memorial and the surrounding garden are open to the public and are illuminated at night by torches. Many Vulcans use the park for meditation or silent contemplation at all hours of the day and night, and visitors are asked to observe proper decorum at all times.

▲ Interplanetary Wildlife Preserve

For centuries, Vulcans have abstained from the exploitation of animals, and the Vulcan Science Academy has been a prime mover in the identification and preservation of endangered species and ecosystems on numerous Federation worlds. Advances in terraforming and genetic modification have assisted these efforts, and the Academy is at the forefront of such initiatives. Situated on a parcel of land south of the city that encompasses 57 square kilometers and features its own lake as well as climate-controlled habitats, the Academy's preserve annex provides visitors with a close look at wildlife from dozens of planets. The preserve is one of only two facilities on Vulcan where you can see everything from graceful yet fierce *shavokh* birds to small, adorable *aylakim*, which seem to thrive on the attention of observers. You can even venture into a cave that's home to a family of *lanka-gar*, the nocturnal predatory birds that live and hunt in the wastelands of Vulcan's Forge. Don't miss the frigid environs of the *zabathu* enclosure, which provides a suitable climate for these beautiful horse-like creatures hailing from Andor. Along with tending to the wildlife sanctuary, the staff here assist in ongoing research efforts to reclaim and restore the natural habitats of endangered animals on numerous worlds. Currently, the facility houses the only known living specimens of *Polygeminus grex*, which was believed to have been rendered extinct at the end of the previous century when the Klingon Empire destroyed its home planet, Iota Geminorum IV. Discovered by a Starfleet vessel in 2373, these "tribbles" were brought to the conservatory and genetically modified in order to curtail their extraordinary breeding tendencies. Efforts are still under way to find a world suitable for this species before restoring their prodigious reproductive properties.

## T'Plana-Hath Historical Museum

Named for one of Vulcan's principal philosophers, this is perhaps the city's most visited museum and the closest counterpart to Earth's Smithsonian Institution. The five-story archive contains artifacts, documents, and other items tracing Vulcan's long, often conflicted history, beginning thousands of years ago and progressing to noteworthy events of recent decades. Within, housed in its own gallery, is the spacecraft named for T'Plana-Hath, which carried Vulcans to Earth more than three centuries ago in order to make first contact with humanity. Holographic re-creations of this milestone and other historical events add to the immersive nature of the museum's exhibits. Guided tours reach capacity early, so plan accordingly.

## ▼ Vulcan Science Academy

Known throughout the Galaxy as one of the Federation's premiere learning institutions, the Vulcan Science Academy has stood as a bastion of knowledge for nearly two millennia. Repurposed from the abandoned ruins of a once mighty fortress, the academy began as a refuge for the first Vulcan high masters as they sought to spread the philosophy of embracing logic over emotion. Today, it boasts one of the Federation's most demanding university curriculums and is a preeminent research center. Visitors are welcome, and guided tours are available during daylight hours. If *kal-toh*'s your game, you'll want to plan your visit to coincide with the Academy's annual tournament, which attracts competitors at all levels from worlds throughout the Federation and beyond.

## 🛍 SHOPPING AND ENTERTAINMENT

ShiKahr boasts several popular shopping areas. While the Multicultural Mercantile District is a prime destination, don't let that keep you from the host of smaller, less trafficked marketplaces to be found throughout the city.

Local eateries are interspersed with an expansive assortment of culinary and artistic fare from dozens of worlds, making the district one of the city's premier dining and nightlife destinations. There are even several restaurants offering fusion cuisine, combining distinctly Vulcan offerings with dishes and ingredients from several of the other planets represented in the district.

After dinner, take a stroll through the entertainment quarter and get your fill of live music and street theater. Like everything else in the district, these offerings feature local and outworlder performers, though even the term "local" gets blurred here when we're talking about the third- and fourth-generation non-Vulcans who call ShiKahr home.

# Calling All *Kal-toh* Players!

Forget three-dimensional chess, poker, or even Fizzbin! True gamesters know that a greater challenge comes from channeling one's intellect toward finding the seeds of order in the midst of profound chaos. No other game offers such a formidable trial as *kal-toh*, the ancient Vulcan game of strategy. For millennia, *kal-toh* has challenged the planet's foremost minds, and each year the Vulcan Science Academy's annual interplanetary *kal-toh* tournament attracts players from numerous worlds, each of them seeking to pit themselves against the game and one another. Though the tournament is open to competitors of all skill levels, only the most accomplished players will advance to the championship round, where the final game can last for days. Do you have what it takes to win it all? Contact the tournament's liaison office on the academy campus for more information.

## ▼ Multicultural Mercantile District

Initially a small collection of restaurants and shops intended to cater to non-indigenous embassy employees and the Starfleet personnel stationed here, the Multicultural Mercantile District has expanded and evolved to become a hub of dining and entertainment for locals, transplants, and tourists alike. It's here that you'll discover a wondrous assortment of local fashion items and cuisine, as well as all manner of handcrafted art and gifts. For example, *Dr'thelek silk*, which cannot be synthesized via replicators and is renowned for its resilience and spectrum of brilliant colors, is a prized material used in the creation of Vulcan clothing. The material is not exported; the only way to obtain dr'thelek silk is to buy it on Vulcan. Similarly, Vulcan's volcanic rock harbors an unmatched beauty that is channeled into the creation of sculptures and other gifts that you'll find nowhere else. As for entertainment, don't let Vulcans fool you with their stoic nature. Like everything else, they approach the performing arts with a drive for perfection. This has produced some of the most complex and beguiling musical pieces you're likely to experience. There is no shortage of live performances in the city, delivered by Vulcan's legions of artists, authors, and poets. Additionally, ShiKahr's diverse population has seen generations of non-Vulcans born and raised here contribute to a marvelous variety of performing arts, from live music to stage and dance shows to holographic cinema. You'll also find that competitive sports and gaming are popular in ShiKahr, and everything from *kal-toh* to three-dimensional chess to Texas Hold'em poker has at least one tournament held here each year.

# DON'T MISS: ShiKahraoke

Like nothing else on the planet, the ShiKahraoke club is one of the Multicultural Mercantile District's most popular magnets for tourists who want to stretch their vocal chords while enjoying a night on the town. Though the club originally catered exclusively to outworlder residents and visitors, don't be surprised to see locals trying their hand at singing timeless classics and current hits. Nothing compares to hearing a Vulcan sing a twentieth-century Earth hit, like "You've Lost That Lovin' Feeling." ShiKahraoke's musical selection is unparalleled, and you may find yourself sharing the stage with T'pril or one of the many other professional recording artists who like to surprise weekend audiences with their own bit of impromptu entertainment.

**SHiKAHRAOKE**

## Subspace

While Vulcan music and performance art tend to be rather reserved, ShiKahr's multicultural allure has seen the planet's nightlife scene grow in recent years to rival that of Earth or Risa. Designed like a concert hall, Subspace's interior reflects its status as one of the planet's hottest modern dance destinations. There is no one musical focus, with the owners welcoming live bands and playing recorded classic and contemporary offerings from around the planet and beyond. That said, if you're not a fan of eccentric musical styles like Sinnravian drad, you'll want to pass on the Battle of the Bands live competitions held every Thursday night.

## ShiKahr Interplanetary Arts Festival

Thousands of visitors descend upon this weeklong gala that showcases the works of local and new artisans of every stripe. Music, live theater, literature, and crafts are just some of what you'll find as you walk the festival grounds. Many artists debut their latest works here, including one of the planet's most revered players of the Vulcan lute, S'tana. Much like the harp from Earth, this musical instrument takes years of practice to master, and S'tana has been regaling audiences for decades with his singular blend of traditional and contemporary musical flair. Though he eschews publicity while living alone in the L-langon Mountains, S'tana emerges from seclusion each year for the festival, to the delight of devoted fans.

## 🍽️ DINING AND NIGHTLIFE

Offering a smorgasbord of local and off-world cuisine, ShiKahr caters to the strict vegetarian diet observed by most Vulcans while providing no shortage of options for tourists and permanent outworlder residents, as well as Starfleet and civilian diplomatic personnel stationed on the planet. Finding something to eat or just a place for a relaxing drink is easy anywhere in the city, but the broadest selection of restaurants, bars, and nightclubs is located in the vibrant Multicultural Mercantile District. No matter your taste in dining or after-hours pursuits, the district is the destination of choice for many tourists when visiting ShiKahr.

### T'vela Sochya

More than a dozen vendors from around the planet come together at T'vela Sochya to create a zesty blend of culinary delights showcasing the very best of local cuisine. *Adronn feltara*, *m'lu*, and *farr-kahli* are among the most popular dishes, in keeping with the Vulcan custom of adhering to a strict vegetarian diet. Pick your favorite or enjoy samples from each of the world-class chefs on hand to dazzle you with their unmatched talents.

### Edrann

You could order something else, but locals as well as outworlders come here for the signature *kahri-torrafeiaca*, a fusion of Vulcan, Rigellian, and Earth vegetables. Yes, it's delicious. Edrann doesn't accept reservations, so expect to wait on weekends.

## DON'T MISS:
### THELIN'S CROSS-TEMPORAL TAVERN

Official records list the proprietor of this popular district bar as an Andorian expatriate, but ask any of the regular patrons, and they'll tell you a different story. Local folklore holds that Thelin came to Vulcan via a doorway through time. In business for decades, though no one seems to know when the owner arrived, Thelin's bar is a favorite watering hole for Starfleet personnel. The walls are covered with all manner of memorabilia and keepsakes left behind by Starfleet officers dating back two centuries. Tourists often pack the bar on weekends, but locals tend to avoid it in favor of more conservative environs. Don't leave without trying a mug of Thelin's own signature microbrew, "Yesteryear."

## Quark's Bar, Grill, Gaming House, and Holosuite Arcade

What began as a single-proprietor club on a Cardassian space station decades ago has in recent years become a full-blown franchise, with locations on more than eighty different planets. There are a number of Quark's restaurants in Vulcan's larger population centers, each offering similar menu selections as well as casino gaming and holosuites. Individual outlets offer merchandise and souvenirs exclusive to that location, but word to the wise: Don't try to steal the menus. Replicas are available at the gift shop.

# 🛏 LODGING

Hotels are abundant throughout the city, though those looking to escape Vulcan's intemperate climate are best served by one of the Multicultural Mercantile District's numerous hotels designed with all manner of outworlder species in mind. Several of the establishments mimic Vulcan architecture, as seen in numerous ancient shrines and other structures of cultural significance, and offer a genuine traditional flair. There are also a few all-inclusive resorts, some of which feature casinos catering to tourists who want to mix a bit of local atmosphere with some familiar creature comforts.

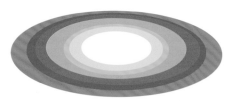

## Firr'creeta ShiKahr

Located downtown and a stone's throw from the city's best dining and shopping areas, this luxurious hotel features a long list of amenities. Its circular design encloses a trio of natural hot springs of the sort Vulcans have long incorporated into holistic healing practices and used as a way to relax the body and mind before meditation. Water travels via underground channels from Vulcan's Fire Plains to feed the hotel's four pools. The therapeutic waters also supply the hotel's award-winning spa. The hotel's service is first-rate from the top down, routinely placing the Firr'creeta on numerous "best of" lists. Regional and outworlder cuisine are in ample supply at the hotel's main restaurant, while satellite cafes, coffee shops, and a wine bar offer their own menus and libations.

## ShiKahr Pinnacle Downtown Hotel

Located less than a kilometer from Embassy Row, this hotel is popular with visiting VIPs and other diplomatic personnel. Its prime location also makes it a convenient home base for tourists wishing to spend an extended stay in the city. The building straddles the Sirakal Canal, allowing visitors access to the hotel via one of the numerous computer-guided gondolas that traverse the waterway snaking around and through the city. Keep your eyes out for o'ktath, gentle dolphin-like mammals, that travel the canal in schools and will swim up to your gondola looking for attention. Though the species was hunted to extinction more than a thousand years ago, modern genetic engineering has allowed o'ktath to be reintroduced in limited numbers via cloning. Their diet is strictly regulated by veterinarians from the Vulcan Science Academy, so please do not feed the o'ktath!

### ▲ Lucky Latinum Lagoon Resort

This little slice of Ferenginar is located on the city's outskirts, with the entire resort contained within its own climate-controlled habitation dome. While the resort caters to Ferengi working or visiting their embassy, all species are welcome. Guests can expect to be treated like the Grand Nagus himself for the duration of their stay. The hotel's central attraction is its three-story casino featuring the latest table and interactive computer games of chance. Dom-jot, dabo, and poker tournaments are frequent events, attracting players from numerous worlds.

# LAKE YURON

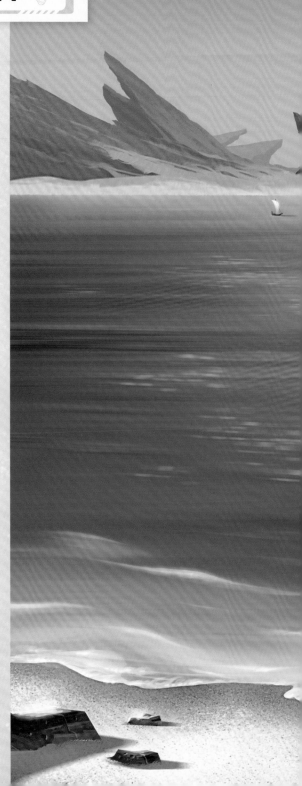

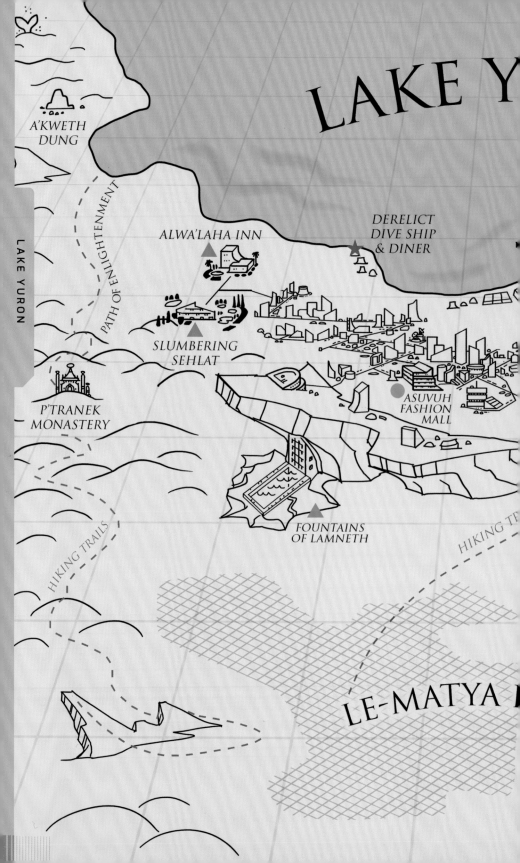

LAKE Y

A'KWETH
DUNG

PATH OF ENLIGHTENMENT

LAKE YURON

ALWA'LAHA INN

DERELICT
DIVE SHIP
& DINER

SLUMBERING
SEHLAT

P'TRANEK
MONASTERY

ASUVUH
FASHION
MALL

FOUNTAINS
OF LAMNETH

HIKING TRAILS

HIKING TR

LE-MATYA

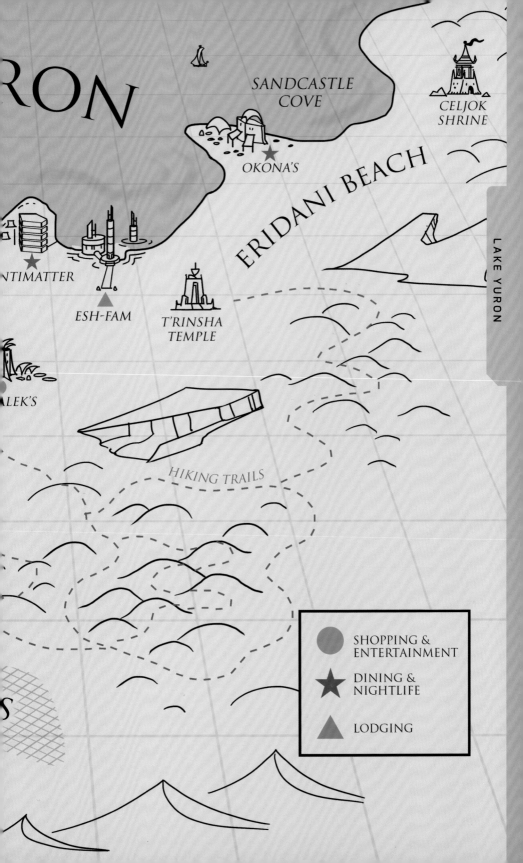

RON

SANDCASTLE
COVE

CELJOK
SHRINE

OKONA'S

ERIDANI BEACH

LAKE YURON

NTIMATTER

ESH-FAM

T'RINSHA
TEMPLE

ALEK'S

HIKING TRAILS

SHOPPING &
ENTERTAINMENT

DINING &
NIGHTLIFE

LODGING

LOCATED WITHIN THE PROVINCIAL LIMITS OF SHIKAHR, the Lake Yuron region has evolved into one of Vulcan's most popular vacation destinations. Once a small settlement dedicated to agriculture and holistic medicine, this once quiet community's beautiful beaches and resorts have made it a target for tourists from throughout the Alpha Quadrant. Tranquil daytime pursuits are balanced against a high-energy nightlife, which makes Lake Yuron a favored getaway locale for university students and Starfleet Academy cadets, especially during the annual *uzhaya wak-krus*, or "season of renewal," which is roughly equivalent to "spring break" on Earth, though far less outlandish. Members of other species who call Vulcan home are also attracted to the lake and the small yet energetic city that has grown up around it, but don't be surprised to see a number of locals enjoying the lively atmosphere.

One of the few sizable bodies of water on Vulcan, Lake Yuron spans an area of more than eighty thousand square kilometers and is fed by an expansive system of underground rivers. Most of the region's major villages and other settlements occupy the area along the lake's southern edge, though there are several smaller settlements and monasteries scattered along the shore and in the neighboring foothills. The region plays host to several festivals and other events throughout the year, so plan your trip accordingly, as resorts and hotels fill up quickly.

Once you arrive via air or ground transportation, the fastest and most enjoyable way to get anywhere on or near the lake is by boat. Ferries run around the clock on regular schedules to a dozen major hubs and minor harbors. Private transportation with optional chauffeurs is also available. Among the most popular boats are those guided by scholars from the nearby P'Tranek Monastery. Despite the availability of transporters, the lake still supports an extensive shipping industry, which serves several of the smaller settlements and monasteries where the use of modern technology is restricted or sometimes prohibited.

Trails and paths connect most of the southern boundary's major points of interest, as the region's original layout was designed to accommodate walking and other self-propelled personal conveyances. This sensibility has remained a priority even as the region continues to expand and evolve to welcome an ever-growing tourist clientele.

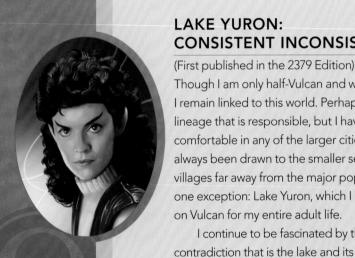

## LAKE YURON: CONSISTENT INCONSISTENCY

(First published in the 2379 Edition)

Though I am only half-Vulcan and was not born here, I remain linked to this world. Perhaps it is my mixed lineage that is responsible, but I have never felt comfortable in any of the larger cities. Instead, I have always been drawn to the smaller settlements and villages far away from the major population centers, with one exception: Lake Yuron, which I have called my home on Vulcan for my entire adult life.

I continue to be fascinated by the inherent contradiction that is the lake and its surrounding regions. Large inland bodies of water are rare on Vulcan, of course, so it makes sense that the lake would attract natives as well as outworlders. One would think this mixture of cultures would provoke all manner of disputes, but, like the residents of ShiKahr and other metropolitan areas, the people of the lake region have found their own sense of community. This does not preclude a healthy dose of otherworldly diversity and the unpredictability that accompanies such variety, which for me is the lake region's greatest appeal.

—Captain Saavik

One thing that surprises many visitors to Lake Yuron is the number of businesses operated by Vulcans. It may seem very much at odds with their lifestyle for the locals to be supporting the vast number of frivolous pursuits found here, but many of the region's best restaurants, popular bars, and hottest nightspots are run by locals.

### Beach Volleyball

Variations of this sport exist on numerous worlds, though it is most popular on Earth, Pacifica, and Risa. Like the courts on other planets in the tour circuit, Vulcan courts are designed so that each half accommodates the natural gravity and atmospheric requirements of individual players. A force field serves as the net at center court, and the ball is equipped with gravity sensors that alter its mass as it passes back and forth across the net. In recent years and with the resurgence of the Interstellar Association of Volleyball Professionals, the Eridani Beach Open has become one of the most exciting stops on the beach volleyball tour. The beach perennially ranks among the top five locations for tournament play, beating out such venues as Risa, Argelius, and Nimbus III. And don't underestimate the locals: Vulcans are some of the best players on the tour and, as with anything else, they play sports with cool, logical precision, combining superior athleticism with unerring strategy. If you're lucky enough to be here when a tournament's in town, don't miss out. It'll be love at first spike.

### ▼ Celjok Shrine

Vulcan historians cannot say with any certainty how long the ruins of this once magnificent structure have stood on the lake's southeastern shore. Myths and legends describe a shrine serving as a sanctuary thousands of years ago for clerics and other religious leaders fleeing the tyrannical rule of ancient Vulcan warlords. What remains of the structure has been deemed a protected historical site, overseen by the Vulcan Science Academy as archaeologists continue to study the ruins and other excavated artifacts.

▶ **Eridani Beach**

The largest and most popular of the
three beach areas at Lake Yuron,
Eridani's fine pearl-white sand stretches
nearly 5 kilometers around the lake's
southeastern edge. The ruins of the
ancient T'rinsha temple mark the
beach's western boundary. Dating
back more than one thousand years,
the temple once served as a haven
for a long-extinct religious sect, the
Krah'jehl, whose members worshipped
Vulcan's sun, 40 Eridani A. The ruins are
accessible to visitors during daylight

hours, and several regional companies offer guided tours. Sandcastle Cove,
the beach's primary gathering spot, attracts heavy traffic from boats that drop
anchor at the inlet's outer boundary. During the height of tourist season, it's not
uncommon to see hundreds of boats floating offshore. Come ready to enjoy full
days of sun and fun before darkness falls and the party really starts.

## Golf

Yes, Vulcans like *kal-toh*, but they also enjoy a rousing game of golf, perhaps
owing to the game's deliberate strategy and the skill required to navigate some
of the planet's more difficult and even treacherous courses. It's a mystery to us,
too, but Vulcan is home to many of the finest players in the quadrant. Le-matya
Flats is designed with an unrivaled aesthetic beauty and is also one of the most
intimidating courses on the professional circuit. Dense forests and rolling dunes
conspire with water and lava hazards to create a series of increasingly daunting
blind shots that can challenge even the most experienced players. Outworlders
from lighter gravity worlds may require a brief period to acclimate to the game
as played on Vulcan, though anti-grav clubs and balls are available to help over-
come this obstacle.

## Hiking

Rivaled only by Vulcan's Forge, Lake Yuron offers one of the most diverse hiking
environments on the entire planet. A number of the trails here are thousands of
years old, connecting the lake to inland ruins and several smaller villages, and
many of the paths still contain paving stones placed there millennia ago during
the Age of Antiquity. You'll want to consult with an experienced guide before
setting off on your own, as several of the inland villages aren't welcoming to
outworlder visitors.

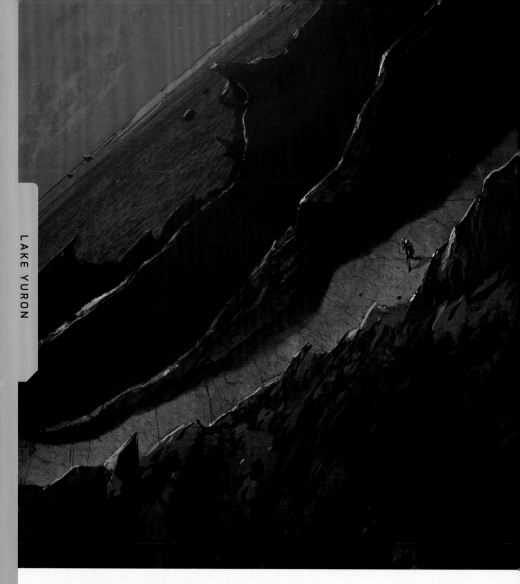

# DON'T MISS:
## THE PATH OF ENLIGHTENMENT

This well-worn trail snakes down from the hills along the lake's southwestern edge to a small cove that is shielded by natural rock formations save for a small passage accessible only to smaller waterborne craft. In ancient times, Adepts—Vulcan acolytes who had attained *kolinahr*, or the successful purging of all remaining emotions in favor of total logic—would follow the path from the P'Tranek Monastery, located in the foothills above the lake, and use the long walk to free their minds and prepare for meditation after bathing in Yuron's purifying waters. The path features numerous etchings and paintings on the hillsides and other rock formations, each depicting legends and folklore dating back thousands of years. One such illustration even shows the acolytes mind melding with *o'ktath*, *i'teth*, and other underwater denizens.

### ▼ Petrified A'kweth Dung

We couldn't resist including this small, out-of-the-way exhibit, which you'll find at the far end of Eridani Beach. *A'kweth*, known to locals as "underliers," are large, whalelike creatures that dwell beneath the sands of Vulcan's deserts. Many scientists believe the animals evolved from an earlier life form that swam in the lake or perhaps even the Voroth Sea. Sightings are rare, as is finding any real proof of their existence. Leave it to the enterprising townspeople of Lake Yuron to make available the only known verified specimen of petrified underlier dung, authenticated by the Vulcan Science Academy. You'll find no finer holophotographic moment anywhere in the city.

### P'Tranek Monastery

Plan to spend several hours exploring every nook, cranny, hidden room, and secret passage of this centuries-old retreat for High Masters and their acolytes. For generations, P'Tranek has been a preferred destination for High Masters and other Vulcan elders who desire a temporary respite from the demands of their office. Those who have attained *kolinahr* are invited to live and study here while renewing their mental discipline and bond with total logic. The hot springs beneath the monastery, tucked away hundreds of feet within the bedrock, provide a rejuvenating cleansing of the body and a tranquil meditation space. Outsiders are welcome, but only during specific hours and on certain days. During these periods, visitors are reminded to observe strict protocols so as not to disturb the shrine's day-to-day activities.

### Scuba Diving

Because of its size, Lake Yuron provides ample opportunities for underwater excursions. The area boasts a great number of seasoned dive masters, but if you're here during *uzhaya wak-krus*, you may find yourself on a waiting list. Most of the tour groups offer scuba classes and certification. There are dozens of wrecked boats and other vessels littering the lake's bottom, most of them making for fascinating dive destinations. Be prepared to swim with schools of *i'teth* and other smaller aquatic life, most of which is harmless. Though some species like the *ul'vath* are predatory, similar to certain classes of sharks on Earth, those animals tend to keep to deeper water, and attacks on humanoids are rare. Rumors and folktales maintain that several spacecraft, including a few from unknown extraterrestrial visitors, also lie among the wrecks, though no evidence of this has ever been found, and the Vulcan Science Academy routinely publishes vehement denials of such claims. This doesn't stop adventure seekers from conducting their own excursions to the lake's bottom in relentless attempts to prove the legends.

# 🛍 SHOPPING AND ENTERTAINMENT

While the options aren't as numerous as those you might find in one of the larger cities or other tourist centers, shopping in Lake Yuron still offers a nice selection of retail and specialty stores. The usual assortment of curios and other souvenirs can be found in establishments both around town and along the water. Because the lake and surrounding region is popular with artisans of every stripe, you'll find several shops and galleries displaying their work. Musicians and other performers flock here during festivals and other tourist-friendly events, displaying their talents on the beaches and in the nearby parks. Everything from dueling Vulcan lutists to people juggling ancient combat weapons can be found here. Impromptu street concerts and other live performances are a common sight most evenings, offering an easy way to unwind after a long day on the water. There are few spectacles that can compare to a Klingon street troupe performing *The Dream of the Fire*, *Rock of Ages*, or *Hamlet* (all in Klingonese) in the open-air amphitheater at the head of Eridani Beach.

### Asuvuh Fashion Mall

A two-minute walk from the beach puts you on the stone paths that wind in and around this intimate cluster of boutique shops. The buildings that make up the mall have stood here for centuries, originally serving as a commune for students studying *kolinahr* at the nearby P'Tranek Monastery. Just about everything in each of these establishments is hand-crafted by local and regional artisans.

When you're done buying souvenirs and other mementos of your vacation, be sure to grab lunch at one of the mall's six restaurants featuring the best regional cuisine in the area. There are also plenty of choices for those seeking outworlder fare. *Yonsavas*, a succulent fruit grown in abundance in this region, are a signature ingredient in many dishes you'll find here.

### P'dralek's Last Chance Bazaar

Enjoy the simple brilliance of P'dralek's, one of the most successful retailers on and off planet and the largest discounter of just about anything and everything. Contained within a six-story structure, discontinued clothing, jewelry, home accessories, and personal entertainment are offered at unbelievable savings. The hunt for real bargains is part of the thrill for hard-core shoppers searching through the selection that is refreshed almost daily as inventory is brought in from P'dralek's locations around the world and points beyond. If you're seeking spices unique to Vulcan cuisine, jewelry handcrafted from the volcanic rock of Mount Tar'hana, or Vulcan wines and other spirits, this is the place for you.

#  DINING AND NIGHTLIFE

At Lake Yuron, the fun doesn't stop when the sun goes down. That's when the action shifts to the town's entertainment quarter, where visitors and locals have been known to keep the festivities going until dawn and beyond. While this might not be the best option for anyone looking to unwind after a day packed with sightseeing and other activities, it's definitely where you want to be if you're looking for the heart of Lake Yuron's nighttime party scene.

### ▲ Antimatter

If you're a lover of trendy modern music and pulse-pounding dance, this is the must-visit club at Lake Yuron. Holographic dancers interact with patrons throughout the club's five enormous levels of illuminated floors and accompanying elevated platforms, all of it synchronized to a state-of-the-art sound system. Each floor boasts its own bar featuring the town's largest selection of beer, wine, and spirits. Don't leave without trying the club's signature drink, the *tolik* sour fizz, made from the juices of the succulent *tolik* fruit, that is just as intoxicating as any cocktail you'll find. Trust us; you'll only need one. If you can make it, come for Noncorporeal Night on Thursdays, which has to be seen (or not?) to be believed.

## Derelict Ship Dive Shop and Diner

This small, unique "joint" is housed within the wrecked hull of a centuries-old sailing ship that ran aground during a fierce hurricane. The vessel, one of the last to use steam as a source of power, sat undisturbed for decades when its owners declared the ship a loss, after which an opportunistic Vulcan claimed it and began repairing and renovating it. He added a support structure that includes part of the restaurant as well as a functioning dive tour company and supply shop. The diner's menu is basic fare, but the diving charters include tours of other wrecks claimed by the lake.

## ▲ Okona's Outrageous Emporium

Visitors pack this beachside bar long after the sun sets, continuing the party until dawn. Started a decade ago by a Terran freighter captain who'd grown tired of hauling cargo, Okona's has become a favorite waterfront party haven, thanks to the broad range of live bands who command each of its three stages. One of the lake's best-stocked bars is complemented by a menu jammed with Earth delicacies. If you're going to travel hundreds of light-years for a pizza, this is the place to find it.

# "Spring Break" at Lake Yuron

There are three reasons you may end up at Lake Yuron during the popular *uzhaya wak-krus*, or season of renewal: You want to be part of the scene, you had no idea your vacation dates coincided with this annual festival, or your transportation broke down and you were forced to make an emergency landing.

Despite what you may think about Vulcans and their reserved nature, the locals are actually very tolerant of the behavior associated with this often boisterous season. This is aided by the large number of outworlders who have established permanent residence on Vulcan and operate businesses in the region. Still, visitors are expected to respect the natives.

The lake is a popular destination for university students from numerous planets and, in recent years, has become a favored setting for Starfleet Academy cadets who make the trip from Earth or one of the other campuses. A number of myths, legends, and outright lies have been propagated over the years with respect to what happens at the lake, so let us help with some of the more persistent fables:

**MYTH:** It's total bedlam here. Originally intended as a time of reflection and restorative meditation and exercise at the beginning of each new calendar year, the uzhaya wak-krus has evolved to encompass seasonal traditions from several worlds. The influx of younger visitors, particularly Starfleet Academy cadets and students from universities on dozens of planets, has given the annual observance an added flair. Though partiers are given a great deal of latitude, the constabulary ensures that order is maintained. Don't try to argue with Vulcan cops. If they've put restraints on you, the logical conclusion is that you did something wrong.

**TRUTH:** If you're a student and think you'll catch up on your term papers or other homework during your week off, quit lying to yourself. Don't even bring your datapad.

**MYTH:** The locals hate it. Definitely not true. Most restaurants, clubs, and shops bring in extra workers to handle the upsurge in business. Even the students from the P'Tranek Monastery have been known to descend from the foothills on occasion to partake in the various festivities, though they always do so in a forthright and logical fashion.

# 🛏 LODGING

Hotels are plentiful in and around the lake region. Discerning visitors likely will want to avoid the typical beachfront shanties and smaller hotels with attached clubs or entertainment venues and opt instead for one of the quieter, all-inclusive resorts and hotels situated farther from the water. However, if you're here for the party, there are deals and packages aplenty enticing patrons to the numerous lakeside hotels and inns.

### Alwa'laha Inn

The larger resorts and trendy hotels have nothing on this landmark bed and break-fast, owned and operated by a small, dedicated staff. Traditional Vulcan decor and dining are the order of the day, and guests are invited to help tend the garden that provides the fruits and vegetables for every meal. As one might imagine, this isn't the first lodging choice for your typical vacationer. The inn is also the region's primary supplier of *pla-savas*, a rich citrus-like fruit used in a variety of food and beverage recipes around the lake. For those who might benefit from such informa-tion, pla-sava juice is often prescribed as a fast, simple hangover remedy.

### Esh-fam

Sure, you're vacationing on a desert planet, so why not spend part of that time underwater? This one-of-a-kind hotel situated on the lake's south-eastern shore has three dozen suites accessible only by turbolift as you descend fifty meters beneath the surface. Each room features curved transparasteel windows, which offer unfettered views of life beneath the lake, so don't be surprised by the curious onlookers you're liable to attract. It's not uncommon for families of dolphin-like *o'ktath* to bump their noses against the transparent barriers in a bid for attention. The latter half of the year is when the *kylin'the* bloom. This plant only thrives in or near the planet's few water sources and is abundant in the lake's shallow areas, growing across rocks and artificial underwater structures.

### FOUNTAINS OF LAMNETH

### The Fountains of Lamneth

Ancient architecture merges with modern sparkle to create an eye-popping hotel that commands atten-tion from anywhere around the lake. Taking its cues from several Vulcan temples and shrines, the hotel's marble façade extends to an immense 80-meter pool and surrounding deck. The fountains that give the hotel its name are active all year long and are as unique as the hotel itself, depicting scenes and figures from across Vulcan history. Guided tours take you beneath the surface to a subterranean waterfall and along several tunnels from a tril-lium mine that in ancient times drew prospectors to the region.

## ▲ The Slumbering Sehlat

Located some distance from the madness that can consume the waterfront properties during the height of tourist season, this modest collection of lodges is found in the foothills west of the lake. Given its proximity to the P'Tranek Monastery, quiet and serenity are the orders of the day here, which might be the perfect prescription for visitors looking to refresh their minds and spirits as well as their bodies. Hot and cold mountain spring water feeds the twenty-four natural pools scattered across the property, and the hotel's private botanical gardens play host to flora from around the planet as well as several other worlds. Botanists from the Vulcan Science Academy have achieved a near-perfect harmony here, cultivating a variety of specimens from the planet's different, often disparate, regions. *Adun* cactus plants stand among a field of lush *g'tesh* bushes. *Plomeek*, *gespar*, and *soltar* plants from the garden are used to make soup and other delicacies served in the visitor dining areas.

# DEALING WITH AN UNEXPECTED OR UNWANTED *KATRA*

IMAGINE THE SCENE: There you are, minding your own business. Maybe you're enjoying a nice meal at an inviting outdoor cafe in the marketplace or relaxing by the pool after a long, hot day spent touring some ancient ruins at the outskirts of the city.

Then, one of the locals is suddenly gripped by some kind of debilitating injury or illness, and it happens right in front of you. You've called for help, and emergency response personnel are on the way, but what else can you do? You lean close to him or her, hoping to help in some way, and that's when it happens. The stricken Vulcan reaches up and places their fingers on your face. *Bam!* Your minds are merging, and before you know it, your minds are one.

Mind meld.

*Awkward.*

But, that's not all. When the victim's hand falls away, you suddenly realize it's a lot more crowded inside your mind than it was a few minutes ago. Now, you've got a whole bunch of new thoughts up there, and *not all of them are yours.*

Congratulations, outworlder! You're now the proud owner of a dying Vulcan's *katra*.

Now, you're probably thinking this isn't a common happenstance, and you'd be correct. The transferring of a *katra*—a Vulcan's living spirit—usually happens between beings who are telepaths, but pretty much anyone can be a participant, willing or otherwise.

Once the transfer is complete, you may become overwhelmed with sudden desires to emulate the behavior of the consciousness you're harboring. Go with that feeling. You should also find the nearest law enforcement or government office and explain your situation, as there are procedures for dealing with *katras* transferred into unprepared recipients. The potential good news is that unless you already happen to be there, Vulcan High Masters will whisk you away for a three-day, two-night all expenses paid trip to Mount Seleya, where you'll participate in an ancient Vulcan ceremony, the *fal-tor-pan*, so that the *katra* you're carrying can be transferred to an Adept or someone else better suited for handling it.

Please note that *katra*-hosting is not something visitors should seek out on their own. Almost without exception, *katras* are transferred to Vulcans who are practiced in the mental arts and who have prepared for the responsibilities they undertake. Only on rare occasions has a non-Vulcan played host to a *katra*, and to say that results are unpredictable is putting it mildly. Curious or adventurous tourists are advised to steer clear.

# KIR PROVINCE

M'DARAN
LIBRARY

E...
FO...

JEVO...
KIL...

FIRE
PLAINS

MOUNT
TAR'HANA

T...
N...

PHELSH'T
FORTRESS

K

THE
CAVERNS

SHOPPING &
ENTERTAINMENT

DINING &
NIGHTLIFE

LODGING

KIR

SHIKAHR
(500 KILOMETERS)

KERETAK
GORGE

KIR
PRISON
HOTEL

HISTORIC
DISTRICT

ORIGINAL KIR
SETTLEMENT

PERK
PLACE

DALOREN
MARKET

CITY

HIGHER
GROUNDS

ZETT'S
EMPORIUM

DAILY GRIND

vLIVE

THANOR SEA

OF
ARTS

ADEPTABLE

THOUGH IT DOESN'T TYPICALLY SHOW UP on many travel agencies' top-ten "don't miss" lists, seasoned travelers know that Vulcan's Kir Province is one of the planet's best-kept secrets. Located along the coast nearly five hundred kilometers east of ShiKahr, the much smaller city of Kir and its neighboring network of villages and farms don't attract the attention of most tourists but are actually the ideal setting for those seeking a microcosm of "the Vulcan experience." Tourists who come here are often looking for something different from what they'll find in the larger cities and areas listed as "*the* places to be." There's also been an increase in expatriates from a number of different planets who have come to enjoy living here. Immigration into the area became so constant at one point that the Kir City Council had to enact zoning restrictions in order to stem the influx.

The Thanor Sea provides the region's eastern boundary, while the northern and western borders are dominated by an array of waterless grasslands, which are choked by spiny *wahmlat* plants. These areas can be challenging for hikers and campers, but don't let this discourage you. Once you get past the grasslands, you'll find yourself amid the region's most notable geographic features: Mount Tar'hana and the Fire Plains. Both are frequent destinations for geologists and mineralogists from the Vulcan Science Academy. Prospective treasure seekers often find specimens of kevas, trillium, and even dilithium amid the canyons and crevasses carved millennia ago by lava from the still-active volcano.

**RIDE LOGICALLY**

 **GETTING AROUND**

Expect to find public transportation that's in line with what you'd encounter in one of the larger cities, though the schedules tend to be more structured and limited. Most magnetic-rail lines halt service in the late evening, though taxis can be found around the clock. The city itself is small enough that most points of interest are within easy walking distance of your hotel. If you're truly daring, you can rent unicycles from one of the local merchants. You haven't lived until you've seen a Vulcan riding a unicycle.

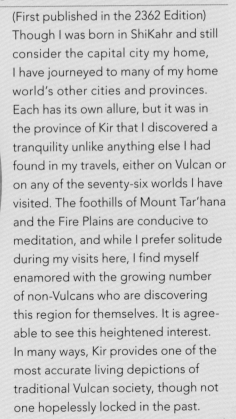

## KIR: RESTFUL FOR MIND AND BODY

(First published in the 2362 Edition) Though I was born in ShiKahr and still consider the capital city my home, I have journeyed to many of my home world's other cities and provinces. Each has its own allure, but it was in the province of Kir that I discovered a tranquility unlike anything else I had found in my travels, either on Vulcan or on any of the seventy-six worlds I have visited. The foothills of Mount Tar'hana and the Fire Plains are conducive to meditation, and while I prefer solitude during my visits here, I find myself enamored with the growing number of non-Vulcans who are discovering this region for themselves. It is agreeable to see this heightened interest. In many ways, Kir provides one of the most accurate living depictions of traditional Vulcan society, though not one hopelessly locked in the past.

—Ambassador Sarek

KIR

## ⟨◎⟩ SIGHTS AND ACTIVITIES

Unlike with the more popular destinations, such as the larger cities or Lake Yuron, once you leave Kir City proper the rest of the province remains, in many ways, untouched by the passage of time. Monasteries and other historical sites are maintained with an eye toward preservation, not just of the physical structures but also of customs and traditions dating back hundreds if not thousands of years. Outworlders are welcomed at most of these locations, but disruptions and other misconduct are not tolerated. Be on your best behavior when visiting these sites.

### ▲ Fire Plains

This is definitely not the place you want to visit if you're looking to escape the heat. Situated to the west of Kir City, the lava fields of the Fire Plains wind through scores of ancient ruins and thousands of years ago provided a natural buffer against enemy forces attempting to advance on the original Kir settlement. Enormous statues carved to depict Vulcan warriors tower over the fierce, intimidating vista, reminding visitors of the planet's turbulent past and Kir's origins during the Age of Expansion. Though the plains can be observed from surrounding plateaus and ridgelines, the best way to experience them is to follow the paths used by Adepts and other High Masters, who often venture deep into the region in order to meditate.

# The *Kal Rekk* Observance and Festival

Vulcans observe the *Kal Rekk*, or day of atonement, by individually reflecting on perceived lapses in logic or emotional control during the previous year. The influx of offworlders to the outlying provinces and cities has seen to it that the occasion now is marked by a variety of festivals and other events. Most of these celebrations are very modest and respectful of the observance's established protocols, serving as a means to honor the Vulcans who have welcomed the outsiders in their midst. If you happen to be visiting during this period, take advantage of any opportunity to participate in one of the ceremonies, as they offer unique insight into long-standing Vulcan customs and societal mores.

### ▶ Keretak Gorge

Visitors are drawn to the hot springs here, which flow into natural pools in and under the volcanic rock, formed after thousands of years of abrasion and erosion from the subterranean rivers running beneath the canyon. Remnants of a long-abandoned fortress bear mute testimony to the wars fought here in ancient times, for control of the springs was a driving force behind the establishment of the original Kir settlement. In ancient times, priests and Adepts incorporated the springs into a host of religious ceremonies including betrothal and marriage rites, inviting those receiving such sacraments to let the waters cleanse their bodies and souls. Visitors are invited to tour the excavated dig site, where historians offer insight into the city's genesis and the battles fought here by rival clans to rule the precious water source. The low-alkaline waters are an excellent restorative for sore muscles after a day spent hiking the Fire Plains.

### Jovorel Kilns

Observe and interact with talented potters and other artisans as they create all manner of functional and decorative vessels, stones, sculptures, and just about anything requested of them. The fires are hand-stoked just as they've been for centuries, and it's rumored that the trio of elder Vulcan women working the kilns have been here all that time. A gallery overlooking the city houses a vast collection of antique ceramics, ancient weapons, and other artifacts recovered from the numerous archaeological expeditions that have been undertaken in the area.

# *Rumarie* Festival

Though the majority of Vulcans have not observed *Rumarie* for nearly a thousand years, those living in some of the smaller villages and settlements outside Kir City still celebrate this rather anachronistic holiday. The festival's ribald, heretical ceremonies and dances evoke Vulcan mores from the Age of Antiquity and have understandably fallen out of favor with mainstream society. Not all of the communities that celebrate *Rumarie* welcome outworlders, so check before you attempt to observe such a ritual.

## M-daran Library

One of Vulcan's oldest historical archives, M-daran was founded nearly three thousand years ago, and its catacombs hold the remains of the first Vulcan elders who called it home. Legend holds that Surak made many pilgrimages here in the years preceding the Time of Awakening, and curators still tend to numerous examples of his earliest formative writings. Reprints of several of his notable texts from this period are available in the gift shop. Indeed, the library's expansive archives attract historians from around the Federation. Tours are offered, though only a dozen outside visitors are allowed into the library each day, so plan accordingly.

**M-daran Library**

## Mount Tar'hana

Visible from ShiKahr, Tar'hana is an active volcano that emits steam on a routine basis along with the occasional lava flow onto the surrounding plains. According to legends dating back thousands of years, the mountain spewed fire and lava at the whim of the ancient god Shariel as a way to subjugate those whose worship he sought. To this day, the volcano ejects lava at frequent intervals, though almost always without serious danger to the city or surrounding region. Scientists monitoring the mountain's activities predict that the next significant event isn't due for several decades, so don't let it impede your travel plans. Visitors hoping for an adventurous hike should be warned that the volcano is inaccessible to visitors except those traveling as part of a formal tour group. Those who partake of such opportunities are likely to observe volcanologists and other geology experts working in and around Tar'hana's enormous crater.

## Phelsh't Fortress

Vestiges of this ancient stronghold still jut from the side of the mountain from which it was carved, facing west toward the Fire Plains. Constructed more than one thousand years ago, the fortress protected a natural subterranean water source that still serves the Kir Province and outlying territories to this day. Centuries ago, the sands bore silent witness to fierce battles, as invaders sought to seize control of the local water supply. Conflicts raged between the armies of various sects. One particularly oppressive tyrant, Sotek, decimated the region and caused many settlers to flee the city for the relative safety of the harsh surrounding desert. What remains of the original citadel is now a national historic site, with curators on hand to guide visitors through the maze of walls and tunnels, which include a lone surviving guard tower as well as ramparts from which archers defended the fortress from attack.

## Vulcan Institute of Defensive Arts

Despite their general pacifist nature, Vulcans are accomplished masters of unarmed combat. Tours of this institute trace the history of personal combat through the ages, illustrating how the martial arts are one of many aspects of Vulcan civilization's more violent early history that was repurposed over the centuries as the Vulcan people struggled to embrace peace and enlightenment. Exhibitions of *suus-mahna*, an ancient unarmed defensive art with many similarities to Earth's jujitsu, take place on the hour, along with demonstrations of the famed "nerve pinch" and the use of traditional weapons such as the heavy-bladed *lirpa* and *ahn-woon* sling. Introductory classes are also available, though you'll have to sign a waiver before you handle any of the weapons.

# Tal-Shanar Observances

Like the *Rumarie* holiday, Tal-Shanar harks back to ancient Vulcan civilization, though it is a much more spiritual celebration that showcases many of the traditions and values that have come to be synonymous with the planet's modern, stoic society. The rites observed during these celebrations are almost never shared with outsiders, whether local or outworlder, and to this day, most of the holiday's protocols are closely guarded by those few Vulcans who still practice them. Those portions of the ceremonies that are open to outworlders focus on self-examination with respect to the planet's violent past.

# ⬚ SHOPPING AND ENTERTAINMENT

Kir City boasts a modest selection of shops and performing arts venues and very little in the way of tourist-targeted souvenirs or curios. You're more apt to come away with a beautiful handwoven scarf or robe, or a book of Vulcan poetry, which is perhaps a good thing. After all, the universe doesn't really need any more Vulcan sand globes (the Vulcan equivalent of Earth's chintzy snow globes).

KIR

## Daloren Market

The closest thing to a dining district that you'll find within the Kir city limits, Daloren Market has more than two dozen different restaurants ranging from chic to seedy. The menus, prices, and quality vary, but if you're the sort who doesn't mind trying new things, this could be the place to unleash your inner foodie. Don't leave without sampling one of the local *t'mirak* rice dishes or *farr-kahli* soufflés. Other delicacies might not be so forgiving on non-Vulcan digestive systems.

## Historic District and Living History Museum

At this popular venue, reproductions of ancient villages, temples, and battle-fields bring the original Kir settlement to life. The district is dedicated to preserving the era in which the original city was founded, with costumed performers acting in the manner of Vulcans from thousands of years ago. Furthering the illusion is the absolute prohibition of any modern technology or anything else that might present an anachronism. Visitors are asked to leave such devices in secure lockers at the district's main entrance. As you wander the streets, you'll be able to observe the performers carrying out everyday tasks just as Vulcans would have done generations ago. Other performers—jugglers, magicians, stand-up philosophers, and impersonators of celebrated Vulcans—entertain patrons while wandering the trails connecting the "villages." Games of chance and skill tempt many a guest, and independent vendors offer a wide selection of period-themed clothing, crafts, and food.

## DON'T MISS: *FALOR'S JOURNEY* SEASONAL FESTIVAL

If live theater and music is your thing, then you won't want to pass up a chance to take in this renowned piece of Vulcan literature performed as it was meant to be seen. Nightly shows bring alive the story of Falor and his pilgrimage across the Voroth Sea and the Fire Plains on his way to Kir and toward greater spiritual awareness. Be prepared, though, as the original tale consists of 348 verses, all of which are included in the performance. Plan on staying after the show to meet the cast and crew.

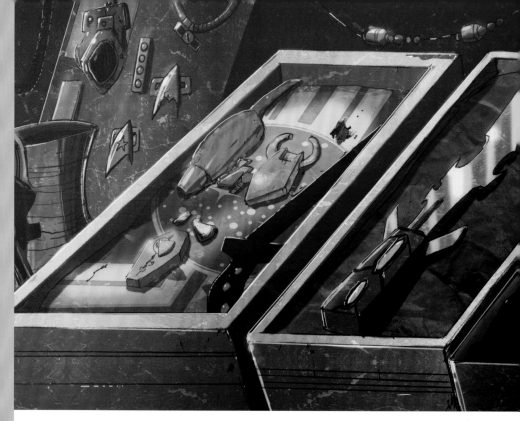

### ▲ Zett's Emporium

The Nalori have been one of Vulcan's most active trade partners in respect to exporting retail brands and opportunities to Vulcan from their home world. Created by Zett, the prominent Nalori fashion designer, this chain of interplanetary boutique shops has several locations around the planet, and it's here that you'll find a vast assortment of jewelry, fragrances, and other gifts showcasing Nalori culture. Only the Tholians produce silks to rival those used to handcraft the apparel that fills Zett's Emporium stores. His material has in recent years become popular with younger Vulcans, who tend to prefer it over the heavier, more conservative fabrics that dominate local fashion, such as the renowned *dr'thelek* silk that is indigenous to this world.

### Clash on the Fire Plains
### Live Performances

A notable, enduring example of proto-Vulcan literature, this twenty-three-part drama recounts the story of the war to control the Kir region, fought between forces loyal to Surak and those of Zakal the Terrible, the infamous yet enigmatic Kolinahru "mind-lord" who opposed the great philosopher. The play is a faithful adaptation of this revered text, performed nightly on the main pavilion in the Historic District. Accurate print and digital re-creations of the original work are available for sale from several of the district's merchants.

# 🍽 DINING AND NIGHTLIFE

If you've read this far and still have doubts, it's true that Kir can be rather reserved when it comes to its nighttime entertainment scene. Locals tend to stick to the taverns and restaurants within the city limits, preferring to retire afterward for private meditation. Meanwhile, tourists and other outsiders flock to the waterfront establishments, where the parties can extend through the night.

### Higher Grounds Coffee Shop

Get your morning started on the right foot with one of the delicious concoctions available here. Whether you like your coffee from Earth, or the Klingon home world, or just about anywhere in between, the shop's talented staff is ready to meet your brewing needs. Forget the replicator in your hotel room; every cup here is brewed to customer order using beans imported daily from more than three-dozen worlds. Vulcan spice tea is also in abundant supply, but be sure to get here early, as the lines sometimes form well before the shop opens.

### T'Mirak Hak-el

Loosely translated as "home of t'mirak," this is the place to come if you're hungry for this popular Vulcan rice variant. Tucked away within the city's commercial district is this collection of more than a dozen t'mirak shops, each with their own spin on this dietary staple. Accept no substitutes; this is the original t'mirak as prepared for countless generations, and these vendors are serious about distancing themselves from imposters. That said, even outworlders have gotten in on the act, setting up their own shops and introducing new recipes and side dishes to accompany the rice.

# DID YOU KNOW?
## KIR'S COFFEE CULTURE

Though Vulcans prefer their *soltar* spice tea, coffee is a mainstay beverage in many areas, and local merchants in recent years have been seizing the opportunity to cater to humans and other outworlders. If you're a visiting coffee connoisseur, then you'll have your pick of no fewer than two hundred different coffee shops and cafes and an uncounted number of mobile or street vendors. Check out some of our favorites from the Kir coffee scene:

- **Perk Place**—A popular hangout for students and artists, this cozy cafe transforms into a bar and dance club after dark.
- **Adeptable**—Perhaps one of the city's most stylish offerings, this cafe resides inside a hollowed statue of an ancient Vulcan High Master.
- **Daily Grind**—Featured in the popular novel *Sands of Vulcan's Forge*, this city landmark is very popular with visitors from Earth and Andor and is one of the few shops offering authentic *raktajino* coffee, blended from beans imported from the Klingon home world.

### vLive

One of Kir's few concessions to the modern urban music and dance scene, this club brings a bit of the ShiKahr high life to the outer provinces. Its rotating schedule features the latest musical offerings across different genres, and the well-stocked bar rivals any you'll find in larger cities. Though aimed at tourists and other non-Vulcans, it's not unusual to see a few locals among the crowd. Be sure to dress your best and be on the lookout for surprise sightings of Vulcan and off-world celebrities, as this definitely is a place you go to see and be seen!

## LODGING

Four- and five-star resorts are notably lacking anywhere outside the city, but if you're open to expanding your horizons, you'll have plenty of choices for experiencing traditional Vulcan living. Rustic lodges and camping are also quite popular with tourists, particularly those planning to take advantage of the hiking trails on the Fire Plains and up to Mount Tar'hana.

### ▼ The Caverns

Excavated from the far side of Mount Tar'hana, this unique hotel features two-dozen rooms, each with its own cavernous ceiling and private spring-fed pool. The lobby has a reflecting pool of its own, along with a waterfall in the center of the room. Private meditation alcoves and a unique zero-gravity fitness center are among the subterranean hotel's long list of amenities, though visitors who don't wish to spend their entire stay underground can also enjoy a pool, garden, and cafe on the surface. Massive geothermal vents route heat from the active volcano, while a sophisticated network of artificial conduits and aqueducts ensure that any lava produced by future eruptions is channeled away from the city's populated areas and toward the Thanor Sea.

## Kir Prison Hotel

Formerly a facility for incarcerating outworlders awaiting extradition after being convicted of crimes while on Vulcan, the Kir prison's origins stretch even farther back into history, when the treatment of inmates was rather less than compassionate. The full gory details of life as a prisoner in ancient Kir are available to anyone who wants to take the guided tour that pulls no punches in this regard. As for the prison itself, it was gutted and renovated in the late twenty-second century by an opportunistic Arcturan who managed to turn the storied property into an inviting, if not lavish, hotel experience. Though traces of the structure's history are apparent throughout—such as its open floor plan and walkways allowing access to oversized guest rooms on the upper levels—this is not a kitschy themed hotel. However, there's one exception—if you're game, three of the prison's original solitary confinement cells are available to single travelers or couples who don't mind snuggling.

## ▶ Selota

Looking for a healthy dose of contemporary flair mixed with tradition? Try this lodge fashioned from a five-hundred-year-old temple that now features all manner of modern appointments and conveniences. Each of the fifty rooms offers a private balcony with outdoor bath and a magnificent view of Keretak Gorge and the Fire Plains. A *pon farr* suite, exclusive to this hotel, features nonbreakable furniture and fixtures to facilitate post-wedding "activities," while reducing the odds of property damage and personal injury. Within walking distance are the ruins of the Ebe'lor Fortress, the site of one of the final battles between forces loyal to Surak and those who one day would flee the planet as part of the Sundering. Thousands of natives left Vulcan in the wake of this schism, spending years in space before eventually founding the Romulan Empire.

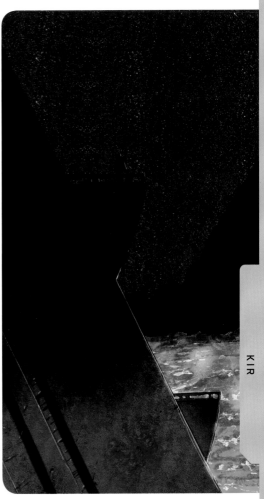

# RAAL

# RAAL

S'LIYATOK
TEMPLE

SEHLAT
ROCK

ZAK
MUSE

EXTRATERRESTRIAL
CRASH SITE

T'PRAN'S
MARKET

RAAL CRATER

KIVA

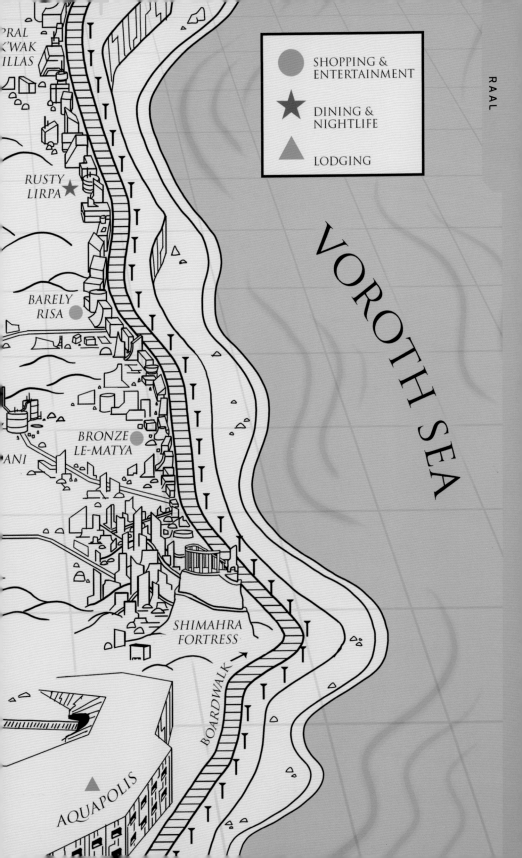

SPRAL
K'WAK
ILLAS

RUSTY
LIRPA ★

BARELY
RISA ●

ANI

BRONZE ●
LE-MATYA

SHIMAHRA
FORTRESS

BOARDWALK →

▲ AQUAPOLIS

RAAL

VOROTH SEA

SHOPPING &
ENTERTAINMENT

★ DINING &
NIGHTLIFE

▲ LODGING

VULCAN BOASTS NUMEROUS COASTAL CITIES that are a natural attraction for visitors who wish to spend their vacation relaxing on a beach. Though not nearly as big or populous as ShiKahr or even Kir, the Raal Province is still of interest to tourists as well as archaeologists. Rather than a single concentrated population center, Raal is instead a hodgepodge of communities situated on the western shores of the Voroth Sea, which shares some similarities with its counterpart on the sea's eastern edge, T'Paal. Several areas along the coast feature ruins and other remnants of ancient Vulcan history, dating back to a time when the famed philosopher T'Plana-Hath traveled the region, recruiting followers to the cause of peace. The province has managed to balance local traditions and sensibilities with the demands of being a popular tourist destination, but unlike T'Paal, Raal is embracing its reputation as a premiere nightspot scene. A recent proliferation of nightclubs and other entertainment venues is starting to receive notice, putting the city on similar footing to Lake Yuron and ShiKahr.

 **GETTING AROUND**

As with T'Paal and other smaller cities, Raal is designed to accommodate pedestrians. Don't forgo the opportunity to explore on foot, as just walking the narrow streets and trails connecting commercial and residential districts is an adventure unto itself. The city harbors many examples of beautiful art, sculpture, and landscaping that can't be appreciated if you're in a taxi or on a mag-rail train. A handful of inner-city areas are off-limits to vehicular traffic, though skiffs and personal aircraft are available for charter in order to reach the outlying areas. A magnetic-rail line connects Raal with other population centers, and satellite stations around the city allow for easy movement.

# RAAL WELCOMES YOU

(First published in the 2165 Edition)

It is a rare occasion for me to return to Vulcan. At the same time, I find that I am frequently answering all manner of questions from shipmates with respect to my home world. It seems that an increasing number of non-Vulcans are interested in traveling here and obtaining first-hand experience of my people and our culture. There was a time when I would have viewed the pursuit of such knowledge as being beneath the notice of many outworlders, namely humans, but I am pleased to have been proven wrong. I am certain this revision in my thinking is a consequence of having lived among them for so many years.

To that end, I often recommend that outworlders in general, and humans in particular, afford themselves the opportunity to visit Raal. My parents and I would travel here for our family holiday retreats. Though now it is common to see humans and other non-Vulcans living and working here, during my childhood, just a few decades following my people's official first contact with Earth, the presence of humans was a rare occurrence. Even then I was fascinated by their carefree nature. They seemed to fear nothing and even overlooked the risks associated with rock climbing or hiking hills and cliffs overlooking the Voroth Sea. I used to consider such attitudes undesirable and even a liability, but time has shown me that humans and other species use this quality to great effect. I am a much richer person for having befriended non-Vulcans of good character, and I believe Vulcan itself has benefited from our relationship with the people of Earth and so many other worlds. It is my hope that you who are reading this will visit Vulcan and come to believe as I do.

—Captain T'Pol

##  SIGHTS AND ACTIVITIES

Raal's active, outdoor lifestyle caters to younger, more adventurous visitors and means you should have no trouble occupying your time here. On the other hand, if quiet and relaxation is what you're after, you'll have no trouble finding that, either.

### Extraterrestrial Crash Site

Every civilization has their own account of how their planet was first visited by "beings from the stars," and Vulcan is no different. According to myth, the inland desert west of Raal is the site of the first reported sighting of an alien spacecraft, more than three thousand years ago. The impact of the vessel's crash landing is said to have created the massive Raal Crater, which remains a popular tourist destination to this day. As the story has been passed from generation to generation, the details have become fuzzy, but the consensus is that a Vulcan warlord, J'Marcel, captured the crashed alien ship and used the metal from its hull to fabricate weapons and shields that rendered his army all but invincible. Though no evidence has ever been found to substantiate these legends, radioactive and metallurgical studies of the crater have yielded mysterious readings that continue to defy explanation. A number of souvenir merchants can be found in the crater's vicinity, and be sure to take advantage of the holophotographic opportunities around the crater itself.

### Antigravity Hiking Tours

Forget "walking tours." Snap on a pair of antigravity boots, stock up on plenty of water, and head out for an adrenaline-pumping "stroll" into the foothills bordering Raal to the west. Experienced guides will lead you on a thrilling expedition along the coast or into the beautiful countryside, which is home to the ruins of an unnamed city that for years has been of interest to archaeologists from the Vulcan Science Academy. Even the clerics of the nearby S'liyatok Temple, whose ancestors have lived here for centuries, do not know the truth of the long abandoned settlement. Earthquakes have ravaged the area, making it dangerous for visitors to approach the ruins on foot, but the antigrav tours allow you to get an up-close, firsthand look at this fascinating and unexplained artifact of Vulcan history.

### Sehlat Rock

Just what you think it might be—this unusual rock formation at the edge of the foothills west of Raal looks very much like a well-fed *sehlat*. Its name was bestowed by an unknown being sometime during the twenty-first century, and the moniker stuck. The rock is a popular gathering place for young people during *uzhaya wak-krus* and in recent years has become a favorite site for music and art festivals.

### ▲ S'liyatok Temple

Like the residents of many of the temples and shrines scattered around the planet, the S'liyatok Temple community has traditionally preferred to keep to itself. However, it joins a growing number of such religious orders that are opening their doors to the public. It's in shrines and abbeys such as this that you'll get unparalleled peeks into the far corners of Vulcan's turbulent past. The monks here safeguard a vast library of ancient texts and other records that chronicle the volatility that gripped the Vulcan people as they struggled to master their emotions and find lasting peace. Open to the public, the temple's library is one of the most comprehensive collections outside ShiKahr or Vulcan's Forge.

### ShiMahra Fortress

Constructed centuries ago to support the efforts of workers laboring in the nearby kevas mines along the coast, ShiMahra originally was a fortress controlled by forces loyal to Sipor, a local tyrant who ruled over the region for decades before he was assassinated by an underling. Only after the Vulcan-Romulan split was the stronghold converted into something more in keeping with the ever-growing philosophies of peace and logic. The settlement was one of many casualties as Vulcans progressed toward an age of industrial and artistic renaissance. Abandoned for generations, it's now privately owned, and most of its structures remain intact. Despite logic and reason being on their side, a few locals still play up the legends of the town being "haunted" as an obvious enticement for visitors.

## World's Largest *Plomeek* at T'Pran's Market

Most everyone knows that *plomeek* soup is a favored Vulcan dietary staple, but few outworlders even know how it's made. The principle ingredient is, of course, the *plomeek*, a flowering plant that grows in abundance in the planet's temperate regions. In most gardens, plomeek are of modest size, but not at T'Pran's Market. This small family-owned grocery store on the city's southern edge has cultivated award-winning fruits and vegetables for generations, and people come from kilometers around to behold the verified record holder for largest *plomeek*. Standing eight meters tall, the plant is definitely an attention getter.

## ▲ Zakal the Terrible Museum and Gift Shop

One of many "blink-and-you'll-miss-it" roadside attractions littering the region, this quaint establishment is something of a shrine to the notorious tyrant, Zakal, from ancient Vulcan history. Zakal's reign of terror against those who sought peace and enlightenment was characterized by torture and mass killings, and the "museum" features artwork and sculptures depicting many of his murderous campaigns. Artifacts alleged to have belonged to the despot and his followers are also on display, including weapons and a handful of torture implements. The tour takes less than thirty minutes to traverse, after which you'll have the opportunity to purchase unique Zakal-themed gifts that we can guarantee can't be found anywhere else.

# 🛍 SHOPPING AND ENTERTAINMENT

Raal harbors an inviting blend of traditional and alternative shopping and leisure pursuits. If you've decided you've had enough of walking tours and other outdoor excursions, the city proper offers a selection of retail shops, theaters, and music venues that let you relax with a soothing beverage as you shake off the daytime heat.

## The Art of Peace

This single-person performance is an adaptation of the book of the same name, written by Surak himself. Narrators stand upon a raised dais outside the S'liyatok Temple's main entrance, orating passages from the ancient tome that provides the venerated philosopher's personal observations.

# DID YOU KNOW?
## UNPOPULAR VULCAN SOUVENIRS

When it comes to buying gifts for the folks back home, it truly is the thought that counts, but that doesn't mean we can't also be a bit discriminating. With that in mind, here is a list of tacky souvenirs to avoid when shopping on Vulcan:

- Anything with some variant of "Live long and prosper" or any use of the words "logical" or "illogical": This includes anything that evokes a double entendre.
- Fake Vulcan ears: Yes, they sell them in most low-end gift shops. No, they don't look good on you or anyone you know.
- Lirpa letter opener: It's funny when it's a Klingon bat'leth, but this is just silly.
- Stuffed sehlats and le-matyas: Not unless the recipient is six years old or younger.

## Barely Risa

Intimate apparel and other gifts direct from the renowned pleasure planet await you here. The popular chain has been expanding its footprint beyond Risa in recent years, establishing locations on many tourism-heavy worlds and increasing its inventory to serve a host of different species. It's definitely one of the few places on Vulcan where you're liable to find a horga'hn, and seldom will you find Andorian aphrodisiacs and Orion lingerie in the same store as you can here.

## Bronze Le-matya Apothecary and Sundries

Named for the life-size bronze statue of a le-matya poised in mid-lunge, this general-purpose "one-stop" shop located in the YonShar village near the boardwalk that runs parallel to the beach almost always has the sort of common, everyday items a traveler needs at some point during their trip. The Vulcan healer who operates this modest establishment, T'Meral, has been here for more than a century, according to the locals. She grows the herbs and other plants she uses to create the pharmaceuticals she dispenses, and several of her holistic remedies are legendary, at least in this region.

# 🍽 DINING AND NIGHTLIFE

Like everything else you'll find around here, the eating and partying scene in Raal is a mishmash of cultures, styles, sensibilities, and attitudes, along with a healthy dose of whatever an opportunistic risk taker can get away with. Raal is the place where you bring your idea after every other place on the planet tells you to go away, and it's all the richer for it. If you don't have fun while you're here, it's your own fault.

## ▼ Club La'Vela

Get ready to have your mind and most of your other senses blown when you pass through the portals of the region's largest and most talked about live music and dancing venue. The club has acquired a cult following, particularly among seasonal *uzhaya wak-krus* enthusiasts who come from numerous planets and dive head first into the club's seemingly inexhaustible revelry. Three concert stages showcase the best new and classic live bands, while six "theme rooms" with their own dance floors offer a rotating mix of popular music across all genres. During the summer, you'll find T'Kelyr and Simal, the "*Mal'neralash* twins," here. Masters of this classical instrument, which is similar to Earth's bassoon, the twins perform as artists-in-residence while entertaining audiences with their unique fusion of numerous Vulcan musical genres. And did we mention the bars? There are seven of them, packed to the rafters with every imaginable libation, and the club's bartenders are masters at improvising new concoctions at a customer's request or on their own whims.

### ▲ The Rusty Lirpa

Opened a decade ago by a retired half-Vulcan/half-human Starfleet officer, this dive is the perfect place to get some decent Earth comfort food while enjoying a game of billiards, darts, chess, or poker. The menu is human-centric, and all entrees are handmade to order, but a replicator offers a host of otherworldly dining options. Leagues take over the pool tables and dartboards at various times during the week, and the bar is a frequent setting for professional poker tournaments. There's also a beach volleyball court out back, though these days it serves as the pit for the bar's trademark barbecue. Contrary to what you might think, it's not just meat that's prepared in the pit, but also a host of vegetable concoctions that satisfy locals and outworlders alike. Don't leave without trying the smoked *ihntya*, which is similar in composition and texture to corn, or the *c'torr*, which, when steamed, becomes even spicier.

## 🛏 LODGING

Raal's accommodations range from plush to paltry, but each has its individual charm. Most of the desirable locations are in the center of town, offering easy access to shopping, dining, and things to do.

### ▼ Aquapolis

"Jaw-dropping" doesn't even begin to describe this incredible synthesis of nature and the work of those who seek to bend nature to their will. Constructed along the cliffs at the city's southern edge, Aquapolis features four hundred rooms, all of them providing astonishing views of the Voroth Sea. About half of those rooms, along with a significant portion of the hotel's public areas, are underwater, with aquatic wildlife visible just beyond the transparent duranium that forms the structure's outer walls. To the south are the ruins of an ancient city, which archaeologists believe was lost millennia ago to the sea as a result of a massive earthquake. Guided scuba tours of the site are available.

### Pral Ek'wak Villas

Set in its own cove at the city's northern end, this hotel is insulated from the hustle and bustle of Raal's active night-life scene by natural lava-rock forma-tions. Bungalows sit along the fine white sand of the property's private beach. Beneath the waves is the cove's natural coral reef at the edge of the Voroth Sea, which is home to a stunning panorama of aquatic flora that makes for truly breathtaking undersea photography.

## ▲ 40 Eridani

Located at the center of Raal's nightlife district, this ultra-modern hotel offers an absorbing lesson in Vulcan's history through archival drawings, photographs, murals, and interactive holographic displays. The hotel is also home to a permanent annex of the Museum of Space Exploration, with exhibits highlighting the planet's role as a neighbor and ally to numerous worlds. Presented here is the story of Vulcan's official first contact with dozens of civilizations. Artifacts in the facility's collection have been gathered over a period of more than a thousand years, brought back by explorers and diplomats who worked to expand Vulcan's sphere of interstellar influence. Included is the azure crystal given to Ambassador T'Lir when Vulcan and Andor Prime established formal relations between the two planets. Perhaps the museum's oddest artifact comes from Earth: a primitive mechanism used to play recorded music. Once called a "jukebox," it was presented by Zefram Cochrane to Solkar, commander of the vessel *T'Plana-Hath*, during its visit to Earth and the first formal meeting between Vulcans and humans. And yes, the jukebox still works!

# PARTICIPATING IN A VULCAN MARRIAGE RITUAL

IT'S ENTIRELY POSSIBLE THAT, in the course of touring one of Vulcan's beautiful cities or other landmarks, you will find yourself pulled into a local tradition. Such occurrences are rare but always memorable.

One of the more familiar ceremonies you're likely to encounter is the *koon-ut-kal-if-fee*, which translates to "marriage or challenge." This ritual has survived for thousands of years, since the times when Vulcans allowed themselves to be ruled by their emotions. Up until a century ago, outworlders seldom, if ever, were allowed to witness such proceedings, which almost always were restricted to family and close friends.

As is now well known, Vulcan marriages are usually arranged by parents when their children are just seven years of age. The couple-to-be engages in a mind meld—a telepathic linking that can even result in the merging of thoughts. Once joined in this way, the pair remains connected on a deeply personal level until such time as they see fit to finalize their marriage. It's during this ceremony that a challenge to the betrothal can be issued, either by another male seeking to join with the female, or by the female if she decides she wants to marry another. If this happens, a *kal-if-fee*, or "passion fight," ensues between the two males, with the winner of the challenge taking the female's hand in marriage.

There have been rare instances in which the female
Vulcan has chosen an outworlder as a challenger to her
would-be mate. High priests and priestesses overseeing
these ceremonies have become more accommodating
in recent years regarding these sorts of deviations from
established tradition, though it's still something of an event
when non-Vulcans find themselves drawn into this ancient
ritual. If you are chosen to be a challenger for the *kal-if-fee*,
the following advice should see you through the ceremony.

- Vulcan customs are not binding for outworlders, so you have the option to decline any offer to participate. Feel free to do so without fear of ridicule.

- Once you're committed, there's no backing out. Also, it's probably worth mentioning that as often as not, your opponent might be suffering from the *plak tow* or "blood fever." This is a symptom of the *Pon farr* biological condition that Vulcans endure every seven years of their adult life. Rational behavior and reason are out the window for a Vulcan affected by the *plak tow*. Prepare to defend yourself!

- If you're not acclimated to Vulcan's severe, arid climate; stronger gravity; and the lower oxygen content of the planet's atmosphere, it's advised that you have a tri-ox compound administered before the fighting starts. You should always consult a physician before taking any medication or before beginning any new strenuous activities.

- Pay attention to the rules of the challenge. The contest is undertaken in stages, each involving a different weapon. The ceremony's overseer will determine the duration of each stage, until one of the contestants is killed during the fight.

- Did we mention that these fights are to the death? Good luck!

- In the unlikely event that you survive the *kal-if-fee* and defeat your opponent, congratulations! You win a new spouse.

- Prizes are not transferable.

# L-LANGON MOUNTAINS

VULCAN'S
FORGE

KAHS-WAN ROUTE

HAULAN

L'JUSA
TEA HOUSE

IDIC
SHRINE

HARMONY
GARDENS
COTTAGES

CRYSTALLINE
ENTITIES

T'GRA
INN

DOCKING
PORT FACILITY

INSTITUTE FOR THE
TRANSMISSION OF
VULCAN CULTURE

L-LANGON

TEMPLE OF
AMONAK

KREN'THAN
VILLAGE

L-LANGON

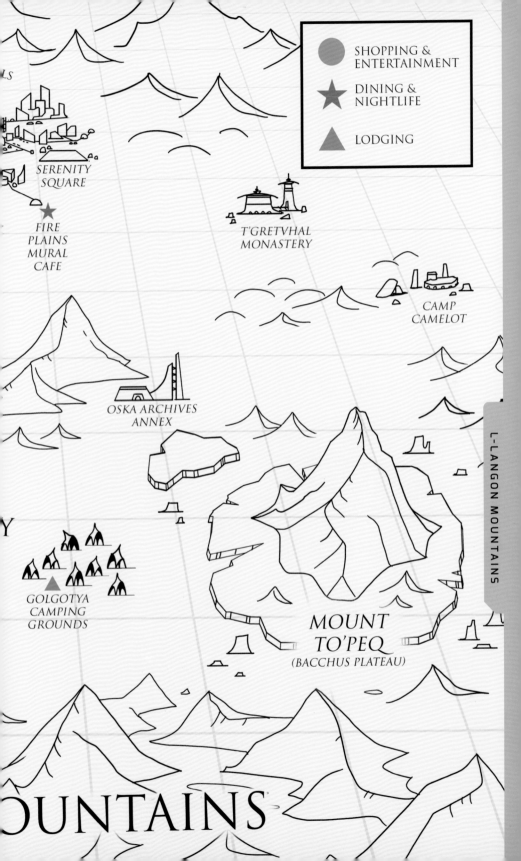

SERENITY
SQUARE

FIRE
PLAINS
MURAL
CAFE

T'GRETVHAL
MONASTERY

CAMP
CAMELOT

OSKA ARCHIVES
ANNEX

GOLGOTYA
CAMPING
GROUNDS

MOUNT
TO'PEQ
(BACCHUS PLATEAU)

○ SHOPPING &
ENTERTAINMENT

★ DINING &
NIGHTLIFE

▲ LODGING

OUNTAINS

FORMING THE SOUTHERN PERIMETER of the desert area known as Vulcan's Forge, the L-langon Mountains are known to be one of the areas traversed by Vulcan children attempting to complete the *kahs-wan*. This traditional rite of passage requires adolescent Vulcans to undergo a grueling endurance test while traversing some of the planet's most pitiless terrain. Those who complete the ordeal are recognized as having taken their first true steps on the path to adulthood. Thousands of advanced hiking enthusiasts challenge the range's brutal topography each year, and the area plays host to an annual weeks-long hiking and wilderness survival challenge modeled in many ways after the *kahs-wan*. Would-be competitors who aren't in top physical condition are encouraged to stick to the villages and other less hazardous points of interest. Outworlders should note that the mountains are also home to a number of settlements that tend to discourage visitors. Check with your travel agent or tour guide for details before setting off on your own expedition.

Far away from the bustling city life that so characterizes the larger population centers, the L-langon Mountains' tranquil setting is also a considerable lure for scientists, historians, and other academics. The Vulcan Science Academy, as well as Starfleet and the Federation Science Bureau, maintains several annexes and other facilities in the region.

## I WAS DESTINED TO LIVE HERE

(First published in the 2268 Edition)

From the time I was a teenager, I knew I wanted to live on Vulcan. The culture here is rich and steeped in an enthralling, often contradictory history. I'm continually fascinated by the methodical nature of the Vulcan people, who approach every task with the same deliberate focus regardless of its scope or complexity. If living among them has taught me anything, it's that patience is not simply a virtue but a survival skill.

My first exposure to this world and its wondrous people was through a chance encounter with Ambassador Sarek. I fell in love with him almost immediately. He'll tell you that marrying me was the logical thing to do at the time, but don't let that firm Vulcan demeanor fool you: I had to woo him.

It's been almost sixty years since I came here to live as Sarek's wife, and my love for this world continues to grow every day. We used to come to the mountains when Sarek's schedule permitted a vacation, and it didn't take long for this place to win me over. Perhaps it's because this is where my husband and my son each took their first steps on the path to the wonderful men they became. The tranquility and simple beauty to be found here has stolen my heart even as it continues to warm my soul. Welcome to the L-langon Mountains and to Vulcan, my true home.

—Amanda Grayson

##  GETTING AROUND

With the exception of a docking facility for aerial craft, the areas open for visitors to the L-langon Mountains do not have mass transportation. Taxis are nonexistent, and Vulcan custom precludes the use of pack animals for such tasks. If you're not using a privately owned or rented conveyance, your mobility will largely be limited to however many feet you happen to have.

## 👁 SIGHTS AND ACTIVITIES

Most of the year, the villages and settlements sprinkled at the base of the L-langon Mountains provide only modest offerings to tourists. All of that changes during the weeks leading up to the Zin'zahn Marathon, when thousands of people descend on the region and take over the limited hotel accommodations and campgrounds. Retail traffic also experiences a sharp spike, as shopping and dining establishments from other cities set up temporary venues here to support the marathon, its contestants, and the masses of spectators and media personnel watching and reporting on the event.

◀ Bacchus Plateau

This expanse of flat rock near the summit of Mount To'peq is a favored gathering place for Vulcan elders along with clerics and students of the nearby T'gretvhal Monastery. It is here that Surak is believed to have faced the most formidable resistance to his teachings, resulting in a brief yet fierce battle with Sobok, a High Master who commanded legions of followers. Though forces loyal to Surak won the fight, he ultimately abandoned this region as he continued his quest. From this elevation, visitors are treated to a wondrous view of the L-langon Valley, with the village of Kren'than visible on cloud-free days. It's a bit of a hike to get here, but the effort is worth it.

### Camp Camelot

The location of a former excavation effort of the Federation Archaeology Council, Site V-271 was established near the outer range of the L-langon Mountains in the late twenty-third century. Archaeologists and historians had hoped to ascertain the location of the ShiGral, a city allegedly founded by Surak as he spread his message through the region. It was believed to be the one place where the great leader's philosophies of peace and logic were never fully embraced, and that the city fell victim to civil war as its people turned on one another. Though the excavation failed to discover the lost city here, remnants of the camp still stand as part of a larger historical trail crossing the planet as the search for ShiGral continues.

### ▲ Flying Tours

While much of the area's mountainous expanse is accessible from the ground only by experienced hikers and climbers, there's nothing preventing you from taking in the area's full splendor from the air. Tour craft shuttle visitors to the high peaks, where long-abandoned castles and fortresses are scattered throughout these remote regions, offering glimpses into the area's distant past. There's still plenty of wildlife roaming the mountains though, including packs of *norsehlats*, which are the area's dominant predators. It's at these elevations that you'll also be able to see flights of wind-riders, delicate creatures that can only survive at the planet's highest elevations. They spend their entire lives consigned to the air, their bodies so frail that they're incapable of even touching the ground. For the most dramatic view, wait until after sundown when the wind-riders' translucent bodies light up the nighttime Vulcan sky.

### IDIC Shrine

This circular stone courtyard stands alone beyond the mountains at the southern plains leading to Vulcan's Forge. At its center sits a massive sculpture depicting the symbol of the Vulcan philosophy "Infinite Diversity in Infinite Combinations." Created centuries ago, the sculpture's origins remain shrouded in mystery. Adding to the puzzle is the fact that the black obsidian rock from which it was carved is not indigenous to this region. How the stone came to be here and who fashioned it into its stunning shape has been fueling debates for generations.

### Institute for the Transmission of Vulcan Culture

The unassuming structure that is home to this centuries-old organization belies the history and importance of the work performed within its walls. Think of it as Vulcan's equivalent of the Federation's Memory Alpha facility but focused on the preservation of Vulcan culture. State-of-the-art computer imaging and data storage enhance the institute's vast subterranean library, which maintains the largest single storehouse of Vulcan knowledge. Visitors can expect a lengthy, comprehensive tour of the facility and an informative presentation about the institute's work and the library it oversees.

► Kren'than

Isolated high atop an unnamed summit, this village is in may ways a "living time capsule," depicting a microcosm of Vulcan as it was in ages long past. In a manner similar to the Bak'u or Earth's Amish communities, Kren'than villagers shun the use of modern technology except in cases of dire emergency. They believe that society's reliance on technology thousands of years ago, particularly that used to create increasingly powerful weaponry, was a driving force in the wars that all but consumed the Vulcan people. Upon founding this village, the initial settlers resolved never again to invite such danger. Everything from the buildings and supporting infrastructure to the gardens, food, clothing, and other incidental needs, is created by hand. Visitors are welcome but only on condition of absolute observance of the commune's rules, which means no holocameras or other modern personal conveniences.

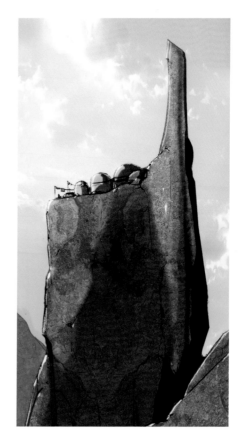

## Serenity Square

This peace park on the front grounds of the Haulan hotel is a favored retreat for locals seeking a quiet respite from the demands of the day. Gardens and reflecting pools are maintained with exquisite care. According to legend, Surak chose this spot to meditate following his battle with Sobok on the Bacchus Plateau before traversing the L-langon Mountains and setting off across the Forge in search of new followers.

## Oska Archives Annex

This satellite facility of the main archives complex in ShiKahr acts as a secondary repository for volumes of official records and other data concerning government matters as well as the personal correspondence and other documents of notable Vulcans throughout the planet's recorded history. Though modern optical media is used to store the voluminous data collected over the centuries, the annex also features several underground levels where original manuscripts and texts are stored. There is a visitors gallery and a brief tour available, but access to the annex's record storage areas is strictly off-limits to outworlders.

## ▲ Temple of Amonak

This sacred shrine is popular with locals and visitors, owing to its prime role in ancient Vulcan history. It often acted as a refuge for religious and political leaders seeking escape from tyrannical warlords resisting the growing peace movement. The temple underwent extensive fortification, becoming a castle that eventually served to repel a number of attacks as the fighting reached its height. Abandoned centuries ago, the temple fell into ruin, until Vulcan High Masters from the nearby village of Kren'than spearheaded an effort to repair the crumbling structures to their former glory. The massive undertaking was concluded in the early twenty-fourth century, allowing the public access once again to this most revered of religious sites. Touring the temple is like jumping back and forth through time as visitors move between modernized interior spaces and the shrine's lower levels, which remain as they've been for centuries.

# Did You Know?
## THE *KAHS-WAN* RITUAL

Anyone familiar with Vulcan customs and traditions has heard of the *kahs-wan*, a rite of passage undertaken by Vulcan children when they reach the equivalent of eleven Earth years of age. It's a grueling ten-day trial in which the candidates venture into the mountains, unarmed and lacking even the most basic survival equipment. There, they must adapt to the merciless environment and procure shelter, food, and water, as well as whatever weapons are needed to deal with the hostile wildlife that lives and hunts on the range.

Multiple competitors can undertake the test at the same time, but rules require each individual to work on his or her own. Even emergency assistance is prohibited. The trial produces numerous casualties each year, and activists have tried without success to have the *kahs-wan* declared a form of child abuse. Though misinformation persists that the test is open only to males, in truth female candidates have taken the *kahs-wan* for generations and often do better than their male counterparts.

While outworlders are forbidden from attempting the *kahs-wan*, a handful of hiking marathons have sprung up in recent years, using the lengthy, treacherous paths traversed by the ritual's candidates as inspiration and allowing non-Vulcans to gain at least some appreciation of the test's arduous nature.

## Zin'zahn Marathon

Using as its point of departure the basic course followed by Vulcan children enduring the *kahs-wan* ritual, this grueling race pushes every competitor to his or her physical limits. Held at the height of summer and in the face of heat so oppressive that even Vulcans are known to express discomfort, runners endure a circuitous course that offers them unflinching exposure to the rugged terrain of the L-langon Mountains. Nearly thirty kilometers of narrow, steep paths cutting through the treacherous landscape challenge even the heartiest of athletes. The marathon has become a huge event in recent years, attracting media attention as well as spectators who pack the area's small villages and neighboring provinces to overflowing. Parties and other events bracketing the actual race generate enough revenue over three weeks to account for 90 percent of the region's annual income.

## ▼ T'gretvhal Monastery

Located in the foothills overlooking the Forge's southern boundary, this abbey was converted centuries ago from an abandoned military fort. Situated along one of the area's few navigable paths, the monastery originally served as something of an early-warning outpost, protecting the temples and other shrines behind it in the event of invasion from hostile forces. Evidence of the damage sustained by the outer walls as the fort's inhabitants repelled attackers is still visible today. The monastery's community is among the more welcoming in the L-langon Mountains area. When you tour, expect to stay for lunch or supper; the clerics will insist on it.

## SHOPPING AND ENTERTAINMENT

You won't find the sort of shopping districts that are commonplace in more tourist-friendly cities and beachfront areas here, but the villages and settlements in this region still offer a variety of charming stores and other retail outlets. Entertainment venues are somewhat limited, though music and theater festivals are frequently staged.

### ▶ Crystalline Entities

Unusual even among the already distinctive selection of retailers to be found here, this curio shop offers exclusive clothing and jewelry creations fashioned from volcanic rock as well as gems and other stones found in and around the neighboring mountains. The shop's proprietors handcraft everything, and no two items are the same. They also carry a large selection of books from local writers and poets as well as music from regional musicians.

### Festival at the Summit

The closest thing to a "block party" you're likely to find in these parts, this festival is a weekly gathering of residents and visitors from all of the neighboring settlements. Follow the winding path to the Bacchus Plateau on Mount To'peq, where you'll find a large campground with stone cooking hearths as well as a larger central fire that is the focal point for the evening's activities. Music and other entertainment are offered, after which everyone is invited to sleep under the stars before enjoying breakfast and fellowship the next morning. This is one of the few events in which the locals welcome outsiders with open arms and no judgments, and it's the perfect way to cap a day's sightseeing.

### Meditations of T'Pau

Live performances of prominent Vulcan literature are common in the L-langon Mountains area, though they're mostly confined to texts from ancient historical figures. Performances that focus on T'Pau are a notable exception and are popular due to her lasting impact on Vulcan society. T'Pau's influence as First Minister helped guide her planet toward lasting relationships with interstellar neighbors, culminating in Vulcan's partnering with Earth, Andor, and Tellar Prime to found the Federation. The Kren'than village plays host to this piece of performance art, in which Vulcan women perform as T'Pau while reciting passages from *Meditations*—her renowned book of writings—and offering unique insights from one of the most celebrated luminaries of the past three centuries. One portion of the performance recounts T'Pau's leadership of the Syrannite Reformation to overthrow the increasingly militaristic Vulcan High Command, which had begun to discard the teachings of Surak.

# 🍴 DINING AND NIGHTLIFE

While lacking much in the way of upscale dining, there's no denying the allure of various small restaurants and outdoor cafes sprinkled throughout the area. Vulcan cuisine will be the order of the day in most places, though a few of the villages also cater to outworlder tastes. If you're hoping to find a bar or dance club that's a well-kept secret among the locals, then you'll be disappointed. With few exceptions, most of the dining and other retail establishments tend to close well before midnight. You might want to bring some books to read in your room or on your balcony after dinner.

### Fire Plains Mural Cafe

An oddly immersive mural covering all four walls of this compact eatery depicts the volcanoes, lava flows, and wildlife that characterize one of Vulcan's most inhospitable regions. The mural was painted in the early twenty-fourth century by a visiting Rigellian artist, based on her visits to the Fire Plains and the holo-photographs she took during her travels. In recent years, the cafe has become a favorite watering hole for locals, be they Vulcan or outworlder expatriates.

### Ba'tak

The trademark Vulcan lack of subtlety strikes again with this simple yet well-appointed restaurant. No replicators are used to prepare the food, and though local cuisine dominates the menu, a limited selection of outworlder favorites is available. Ba'tak (which translates to "tradition") is known for its *bertakk-torrafeiaca* stew, which is second to none in the region. The place isn't flashy, but the ambiance is welcoming and soothing after a long day spent sightseeing.

### L'jusa Tea House

Enjoy morning or afternoon tea at this picturesque cafe near the Harmony Gardens cottages whether your taste runs to local specialties like *n'gaan* spice tea or herbal beverages from your own home world. The shop also sells a rich assortment of traditional confections, and its lunch menu offers a small selection of light dining options. Next door is a *kal-toh* parlor owned by the same proprietor, and it's not uncommon for patrons to enjoy their tea and sweets while taking advantage of some lively gaming.

**L'jusa Tea House**

## 🛏 LODGING

With a single exception, there are no luxurious, all-inclusive resorts located in the region, though several of the villages feature small hotels and cabins or cottages for rent. Do you really need five-star hotel staff service when practically every window has a magnificent mountain view?

### Golgatya Camping Ground

Visitors looking for a break from the usual hotel or inn might like the change of pace offered by this small, secluded campground at the edge of the nearby mountains. Accessible only via the footpath leading into the foothills and through several small villages, the region is the source of many stories and folktales that attract curiosity seekers. Legends tell of voices that can be heard echoing through the hills at night and are believed to belong to warriors killed in battles centuries ago. As the story goes, Tokar, a powerful Vulcan mind-lord, cast their *katras* upon the winds, dooming them to exile and eternal damnation.

### ▲ Haulan

Haulan is the aforementioned only all-inclusive resort in the region. In Vulcan, *haulan* means "reflection," and this hotel lives up to its simple moniker by embodying Vulcan traditions, which means the accommodations are simple while still possessing an undeniable elegance. A tour guide is on hand to illuminate visitors regarding the hotel's origins as a fort constructed by forces loyal to Sobok, a local tyrant who ruled over the region two millennia ago, enslaving the settlers and conscripting all able-bodied Vulcans into his army. Remnants of the original encampment are kept in the property's subterranean levels. By far the largest hotel in the area, Haulan boasts sixty-seven rooms, each of which offers a spectacular view of the mountains and the Forge beyond.

## ▼ T'grat Inn

Formerly a monastery of indeterminate origin and ownership, the T'grat Inn was converted into a bed and breakfast at the turn of the century. According to folklore, war refugees used the original abbey as a temporary sanctuary during their movements through the region as they sought to evade Sobok's legions as well as the despot's unremitting cruelty. Eleven well-appointed rooms offer a calming view of a lazy stream winding down through the foothills. The owners provide breakfast consisting of typical Vulcan fare, though they're able to accommodate many other species' dietary requirements upon request.

# T'PAAL

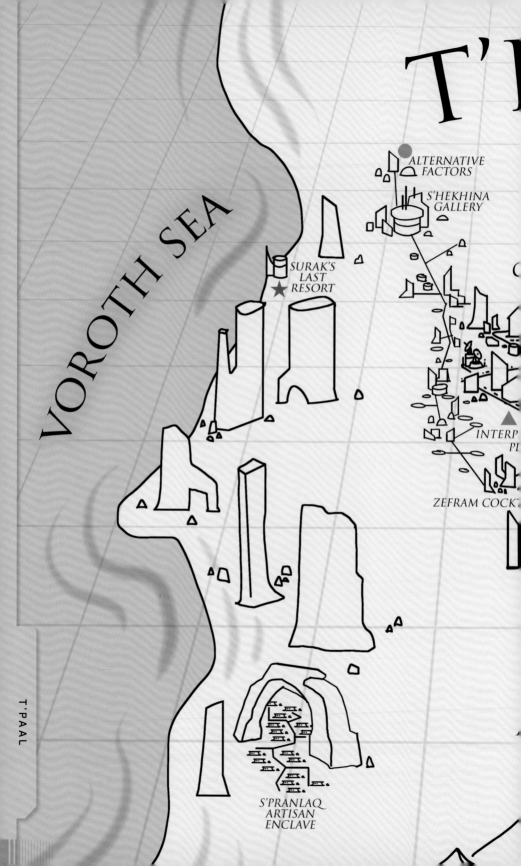

T'P

VOROTH SEA

ALTERNATIVE
FACTORS

S'HEKHINA
GALLERY

SURAK'S
LAST
RESORT

INTERP
PI

ZEFRAM COCKT

S'PRANLAQ
ARTISAN
ENCLAVE

AAL

SHOPPING &
ENTERTAINMENT

DINING &
NIGHTLIFE

LODGING

T'PAAL
OBSERVATORY

NTER

RAU-NOL

VEKLAR
PRISON
MUSEUM

CHAMBER
MUSIC
PAVILION

ALTITUDE

NOLATIHR
PEACE
PARK

LOCATED ON THE EASTERN EDGE OF THE VOROTH SEA, T'Paal has followed the example set by Lake Yuron and other smaller cities around the planet and fully embraced the idea of becoming a tourist attraction. Indeed, the entire area is a regular entry on numerous "can't miss" destination lists. Distant enough from the equator that its coastal location enjoys a temperate climate year-round, T'Paal has seen remarkable growth in recent years. A number of outworlder immigrants and other expatriates have settled here, seeking escape from the more frantic pace of life that so characterizes the larger population centers on their own worlds.

T'Paal strikes a balance between primitive throwback settlement and luxury resort. Its most distinctive features are its brilliant brick-red soil and its enormous rock formations that face west toward the ocean, towering into the sky and standing like sentries guarding the local inhabitants. Viewed by many Vulcans as sacred land, the entire region has long held a well-earned reputation as a destination for mental and physical healing as well as spiritual renewal. It's also a lure for artisans of every stripe.

Though not quite hedonistic, the city's culture is carefree and permissive, fully embracing the Vulcan principle of "Infinite Diversity in Infinite Combinations." In fact, T'Paal has become something of a magnet for the counterculture of both immigrants and locals alike, with most of T'Paal's Vulcan residents having forsaken the usual trappings and mores of their native society. You may very well encounter the occasional local who has cast off even the most basic Vulcan tenet of emotional suppression. If you think a cold, logical Vulcan makes for an intimidating debate opponent, try taking on one who's retained that formidable grasp of unassailable logic while letting his emotions run unchecked. Engage with these individuals at your own peril.

## T'PAAL: CELEBRATING DIVERSITY

(First published in the 2377 Edition)

I sit here, allowing the rays of our sun to warm my skin. It has been too long since I last experienced this sensation. After spending the past seven years with my shipmates aboard the *U.S.S. Voyager* as we worked to traverse the Delta Quadrant and return home, my thoughts were always of my wife, T'Pel, and my four children. Now I am home, and I am once again surrounded by my family.

Though I was not actually born on Vulcan, I have always called the planet my home. The larger cities of Vulcan didn't speak to me; instead I was drawn here, to T'Paal. The ocean appeals to me, though I am never far from the desert's warmth or from the serenity to be found while meditating among the rock formations, which have stood here for uncounted generations. It is here that I met T'Pel and that our daughter, Asil, was born.

At first, I was uncomfortable with T'Paal's unconventional atmosphere, which seemed to flout our people's customs and traditions. Then I met T'Pel, and it was she who helped me to appreciate the city and those who call it home. Though there are those who view T'Paal as being out of step with Vulcan societal norms, in reality the city and its people represent the very essence of the diversity we cherish.

—Lieutenant Commander Tuvok

##  GETTING AROUND

T'Paal is bracketed by mountains to the east and the Voroth Sea to the west. The region's original settlers therefore expanded outward from the original village to the north and south, following the topography, so the city is long and narrow. Because of this, you can expect to do a lot of walking to get from one end of the city to the other. Modern conveyances are prohibited within the city center, and transporters are limited to official and emergency use. Skiffs and magnetic rail are used for tours of the surrounding mountains and canyons. Given the locals' penchant for physical fitness and outdoor activities, don't be surprised to encounter runners and hikers everywhere you go.

# SIGHTS AND ACTIVITIES

T'Paal's embrace of the arts has made it a sanctuary for creative souls of every sort. You can't throw a rock without hitting a gallery, outdoor display, or performance venue. Many of the galleries offer demonstrations and classes tailored to all skill levels, so don't be afraid to partake of everything this welcoming city has to offer.

### ▲ Nolatihr Peace Park

A stunning amalgamation of natural rock formations and precision stonework constructed hundreds of years ago by the region's original settlers, the Nolatihr Peace Park is accented by the wondrous beauty of waterfalls, reflecting pools, and gardens showcasing flora from around the planet. The huge *karanji* cactus plants that grow here were first planted two centuries ago and now soar nearly fifty meters above the park grounds. This tranquil setting is one of T'Paal's most inviting destinations and a popular venue for weddings and other ceremonies and family rituals. Some locals even proclaim that the site bore witness to the first ever *koon-ut-kal-if-fee*, the Vulcan "marriage or challenge" ritual, and ignore all attempts by historians to set the record straight. Artists and photographers find inspiration among the glades and walking paths. It's also a popular location for meditation, and it's common to find people having picnics or simply lounging beneath one of the many trees while reading a book and enjoying the fresh air.

## S'hekhina Gallery of Visual Art

Founded in the early twenty-first century by celebrated Vulcan holo-photographer Selek, this unassuming three-story structure is home to many of his evocative and immediately recognizable images of notable Vulcan women. Selek's granddaughter serves as the gallery's curator, offering insightful guided tours about his work several times each day.

## ◀ S'pranlaq Artisan Enclave

Situated beneath an enormous natural stone arch near the city's western border, S'pranlaq is a collection of modest bungalows and other small buildings connected by cobblestone paths, which wind through the gardens, ponds, waterfalls, and numerous small rock formations that make up the enclave's courtyard. A popular destination for artists from all disciplines, S'pranlaq began life as a commune for disciples of the goddess Akraana from Vulcan mythology, who was the wife of the war god Khosarr. In keeping with their absolute devotion to Akraana, the followers excluded themselves from the rest of Vulcan society, building and growing by hand everything they needed to sustain their closed, self-sufficient community. Though worship of the ancient gods has fallen out of favor, residents of the enclave continue to observe the old customs, maintaining the enclave even while carrying out their artistic pursuits.

More than two dozen shops and restaurants are interspersed with twice that many galleries, and the outdoor spaces here are liberally decorated with murals, statues, and other sculptures and carvings created by the commune's guests. Though Vulcans make up the bulk of the population, it's not unusual to find a few outworlders in residence. Don't miss the live music festivals held each weekend in the village's central courtyard.

## T'Paal Observatory

Even with the advent of satellites, space-based telescopes, unmanned interstellar survey probes, and long-range sensors, there is nothing better than beholding distant stars with the naked eye. Land-based astronomy remains a popular activity on Vulcan, as it is on countless other worlds, and the Vulcan Science Academy operates several astronomy facilities around the planet, all of which are open to the public. The T'Paal Observatory is one such site, situated in the mountains above the city's northern boundary, and hosting stargazing sessions each night beneath the brilliant Vulcan sky. Subspace-imaging telescopes and stellar cartographic holosimulations allow visitors to reacquaint themselves with the universe around them and their place in it.

## ▲ Veklar Prison Museum

A relic of a bygone age, this prison presents a foreboding silhouette against the backdrop of mountains west of the city. While violent crime is almost unheard of on Vulcan, and the modern justice system emphasizes rehabilitation over incarceration and punishment, this was not always the case. Long abandoned as the planet embraced Reformation, prisons like Veklar now stand as reminders of Vulcan's brutal past. Guided tours lead you through a maze of corridors and underground passageways, and there are also costumed performers reenacting a typical day in the life of both the inmates and the guards. Due to the graphic nature of these performances, visitor discretion is advised.

# 🛍 SHOPPING AND ENTERTAINMENT

Unlike many other prime tourist destinations, T'Paal has no centralized shopping district or bazaar. Instead, boutiques, small galleries, and modest retail areas are found throughout the hills and valleys upon which the city is built. Walking west from the beaches, you'll find open-air bazaars rather than the usual department stores or shopping precincts, many of them occupying caves and furrows within the rock. Likewise, amphitheaters and stages use the spectacular backdrop of the city's stone formations or are constructed so that they blend seamlessly with the natural surroundings.

## Alternative Factors

Renowned for its selection of rare and out-of-print books, this quaint little shop has to be seen to be believed. What at first appears to be a single-story structure near the city's northern end actually extends several floors below ground, with every millimeter of available space stuffed to overflowing with vintage tomes. Vulcan literature is well represented, of course, but you'll find everything from classics to mass-market pulp from dozens of planets hiding on the shelves. On display here is the original handwritten manuscript for *The Runes of T'Vish*, the seminal work by renowned Vulcan philosopher T'Vish that continues to set the standard to which young Vulcan adults aspire when honing their mental discipline and learning to control their emotions.

ALTERNATIVEFACTORS

## Mahr-kel-svitan

Every tourist town has them, and T'Paal is no exception. What began as a handful of smaller shops on the fringes of the city center has grown over time to become its own destination. A single street of offbeat, unconventional merchants cater to those looking to break away from the rest of the T'Paal art and craft scene. If you're looking for that inexpensive, inelegant, and even tacky memento for yourself or a friend, chances are good you'll find it here. This is the place where gaudy shirts and *katric* ark nesting eggs come to die.

## Chamber Music Pavilion

At T'Paal's Chamber Music Pavilion, small, intimate gatherings of musicians employ disparate types of instruments—often representing different cultures and musical styles—and play for audiences ranging from the single digits to more than a hundred. One local troupe's nightly performance of "The Journey Songs," which describe the arduous migration of the Eeiauoan people from their ancestral home to their new world, routinely packs the place, so get there early.

### Gad'muf fi'kov

Loosely translated as "festival atop the rock," this gala is held each year at the summit of nearby Mount Amanut south of the city. An exceptional array of acclaimed celebrity artists and musicians representing most of the planet's leading performing arts communities is usually in attendance. Locals and outworlders participate, and the annual event draws spectators from dozens of worlds. Classes and workshops for every skill level invite young musicians to hone their craft while learning from masters. The festival is also one of the few places where you'll see Klingon opera, Earth jazz, Lurian folk ballads, and Arcturian death metal performed in such close proximity, not to mention the impromptu collaborations that get kicked up on a whim.

## 🍽️ DINING AND NIGHTLIFE

Like many cities catering to outworlders and individualists of the sort found in an artisan community, some parts of T'Paal don't even get going until after the sun goes down. Most of the restaurants, bars, and cafes are open at all hours, but it's when darkness falls that the nightclubs come alive, catering to nocturnal fun seekers.

### Rau-nol

In Federation Standard, *rau-nol* means "refuge" or "sanctuary." The city's largest nightclub is four stories of arcade gaming, billiards, dance floors, darts, dining, karaoke, poker, and bars. Two lounges on each floor offer plenty of casual seating for watching the dance action. Though originally intended to draw in tourists looking for something out of step with typical Vulcan nightlife, Rau-nol has grown its clientele to include younger locals who've taken up residence in the artisan communes. The cover charge includes credits for the arcade and other games, and the drinks and food are reasonably priced. Be sure to try the signature *n'gaan* spiced rum, hand-crafted on the premises and exclusive to the club.

SURAK'S LAST RESORT

### Surak's Last Resort

Founded last century by an enter-prising Tellarite with a penchant for flouting convention, this bar-and-grill restaurant is famous for its all-Vulcan staff that takes obnoxious logic and condescension to new extremes while "serving palatable food, temperature-controlled alcoholic beverages, and helpful insights into the lesser beings to which we cater." That means you. If you have a sense of humor and can abide being schooled by your intellec-tual superiors while they feed you, then this is your place. Be sure to check out the gift shop on your way out.

## Zefram Cocktails

Located in the city's historic district, this popular hangout makes no bones about what it is: an Earther joint for Earthers. Owned and operated by a Terran who retired from Starfleet after decades as a starship engineer, this bar is popular with Starfleet and Federation diplomatic personnel. The drink menu is as long as the résumé of its proprietor, and if you can stump them with your exotic drink order, it'll be a first.

#  LODGING

T'Paal's unconventional community and sensibilities are reflected in many of the area hotels. Major chains are represented well enough, but it's the smaller, independently operated establishments that really highlight the city's diverse charm.

### ▼ Altitude Tree House Enclave

Leave it to the Ferengi to spare no expense while devising a themed hotel, and this is one of their more distinctive properties. Not to be deterred by the notable lack of trees in the region, Ferengi business executives had genetically engineered trees imported in order to build an entire forest. One square kilometer of actual forestland sits between the city and the desert plain to the east, with each massive tree towering dozens of meters into the air while boasting its own custom tree house. Several of the tree houses are accessible only by the resort's network of rope bridges and zip lines. No two cottages are the same, and each affords its guests spectacular views of the city and the Voroth Sea to the west.

### Interplanetary Plaza Hotel

Time has done nothing to dull the allure of this historic hotel, constructed four centuries ago. With the continuing increase in tourism in T'Paal, the Plaza has embraced the need to cater to outworlders while still balancing a desire to uphold Vulcan culture and tradition. Located in the foothills east of the city center, the hotel places guests within easy walking distance of T'Paal's numerous dining and entertainment options. Formerly the headquarters of the High Command, the hotel was the site of the landmark treaty that ended hostilities between Vulcan and Tellar Prime during the twenty-second century. The original treaty documents—all 107 densely worded pages—are available for viewing in the hotel's visitor chamber. The chamber's walls also feature a hand-painted mural depicting the planet's history from the Time of the Beginning to its role in the founding of the Federation.

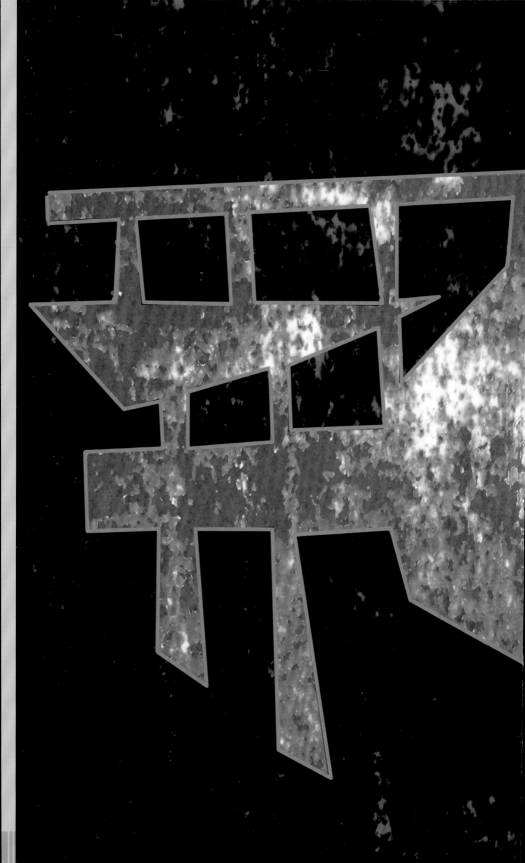

# SO YOU WANT TO PURGE ALL OF YOUR EMOTIONS

SUFFERING FROM ANGER MANAGEMENT ISSUES? Have you ever snapped at a coworker, friend, or loved one, realizing even as the words left your mouth that you have crossed a line? Are you tired of making rash decisions in the heat of the moment, only to regret that hasty action? Want to learn to keep a leash on your feelings, so that logic and reason can be fully embraced? You can—by achieving *kolinahr*.

This isn't some trendy, "immediate results guaranteed" program. Those visiting for only a short time won't find any quick-and-easy methods to achieving this extremely desirable state of Vulcan mental well-being. Instead, you'll have to be willing to sign on for a commitment that might take several years to yield the desired results.

Those choosing to accept the challenge *kolinahr* presents must travel to the Plains of Gol deep within the inhospitable deserts of Vulcan's Forge. There, under the uncompromising guidance of skilled High Masters, students learn to cast off their emotions and focus their minds to achieve total logic. After successfully navigating this demanding trial, students spend additional time achieving emotional closure with family and close friends. Only upon purging these lingering yet still powerful emotional remnants is a student considered to have achieved *kolinahr*.

**Do you have what it takes?**

# VULCANA REGAR

TVI'SOCHYA

VULCAN

J'U
STREE

T'JEREL
GALLERY

MONASTERY
OF SAVAL

SHAUKAUSH

"EPICENT
(ORIGINAL
SETTLEMENT
TOPOGRAPHY

MUSEUM OF
VULCAN-ANDORIAN
RELATIONS

THE LAZY
LE-MATYA

PO
FAC

WORLD'S LARGEST
KAL-TOH GAME

TEMPLES OF
SYRINX

VANIK TOWER

REGAR

DESERT PLAINS

SHOPPING & ENTERTAINMENT

★ DINING & NIGHTLIFE

▲ LODGING

PORT 47 IMPORTS

VIC'S LOUNGE

MOUNTAINS TO EAST

B-JINGLAN AIR/SPACE MUSEUM "BONEYARD"

SPACEPORT

★ LAUNCH COMPLEX BISTRO

DESPITE SHIKAHR'S SIZE, Vulcana Regar holds the honor of being the planet's largest city as well as its undisputed metropolitan heart and soul. Beginning as a simple spaceport complex in an era when the launching and recovery of spacecraft was far more dangerous than it is today, the city expanded to become the center of Vulcan's space-based commercial interests. The planet's oldest and most successful companies and mercantile families call the city home and 90 percent of imported goods come through Vulcana Regar. Many outworlder businesses are located here as well, constituting a hub of commerce unlike anything seen beyond Ferenginar or Arcturus. Perhaps feeling kinship with their more commercially minded Vulcan counterparts, the Ferengi established their embassy here rather than in ShiKahr, and Ferengi merchants operate more than 10 percent of the city's warehouses and cargo processing facilities.

Despite what at first would seem to be a rather industrial milieu, Vulcana Regar still manages to attract tourists and other visitors thanks to its unparalleled selection of retail shops, restaurants, and night spots. As the old saying goes, "Work hard, play hard," and nowhere on the planet is that truer than Vulcana Regar.

##  GETTING AROUND

Public transportation is abundant and convenient throughout the city, and most options are available at all hours. Expect to do a lot of walking in the city's retail and entertainment quarters, but many of these areas feature canopies that block out the worst of the sun, and at night those same shelters become display screens for a variety of light shows and other video simulations. Marked paths guide you through walking tours of the city's historic districts.

## VULCANA REGAR: GATEWAY TO THE STARS

(First published in the 2275 Edition)
Much has been written about Vulcan culture for the benefit of outworlders. We possess a long, often violent history, but it is from that chaos that we have emerged as a people of enlightenment. For many generations, we did not seek to find our place among our interstellar neighbors, but I am pleased to see that from out of our initial reticence has grown a vast cooperative, spanning hundreds of worlds, from which each of us can continue to learn while celebrating our differences as well as our similarities.

None of that would be possible if we were unable to escape the confines of our own world. It is here, in this place we now call Vulcana Regar, that we made our first tentative forays into space. There, we found new friends and allies, and now our lives are forever intertwined with those of other beings on distant worlds.

Vulcana Regar continues that proud tradition, acting as our path to the stars as well as a gateway through which those from other planets can come and learn more about us. It is here, through the trading not only of goods but also goodwill, that the bonds of friendship are forged and continually strengthened.

—First Minister T'Pau

## 👁 SIGHTS AND ACTIVITIES

Despite its seeming emphasis on commercial pursuits, Vulcana Regar still offers plenty for tourists and other visitors to enjoy. History and art aficionados will have no trouble filling their schedules, and there are the usual assortment of quirky attractions that make wandering off the beaten path worth the extra effort.

### ▼ B-jinglan Air and Space Museum and Aircraft Boneyard

Hundreds of aircraft and space vessels accompany dozens of interactive exhibits at this one-of-a-kind repository located north of the original Vulcana Regar space-port complex. While a history of Vulcan aviation and space travel is the centerpiece of the museum, you'll also see dozens of representatives of commercial, military, and private craft interred in "the boneyard," many of them dating back to the first generations of interstellar relations and trade between Vulcan and other planets. There also are a few genuine mysteries to be found here, in the form of a handful of spacecraft that have yet to be identified. The yard's most prominent feature is the *Ni'Var*, a *Suurok*-class starship retired from service nearly two centuries ago. Following the last major battle of the Romulan War, the *Ni'Var*'s captain, Sopek, negotiated the treaty that ended the conflict. The vessel is suspended in the same drydock facility where it was constructed. Force field generators keep the *Ni'Var*'s fragile hull from succumbing to the planet's gravity and allow visitors to tour the ship's interior.

### ▲ EpiCenter

Vulcana Regar's picturesque central square features a number of fascinating older buildings, many of which formed part of the original settlement in ancient times. Clues to the city's past remain, hinting at its genesis as a military outpost that protected the mountain pass to the east. The original fortifications, along with what is believed to have been an arsenal, underground bunkers, and a network of tunnels now serve as museums, art galleries, craft and antique shops, teahouses, and cafes. The memorial garden at EpiCenter's far end pays tribute to the city's founders as well as the numerous battles fought in this region to protect early settlers against invasion.

### Monastery of Saval

Believed to be one of the first religious shrines erected in the region, this monastery has stood unchanged for more than two thousand years. *The Odyssey of Surak*, one of the earliest examples of Vulcan historical fiction, was written here by Saval, a High Master and one of the Surak's earliest supporters. Unlike those at other shrines and historical sites, the clerics living here have embraced and integrated modern technology into their ministry and work. Centuries of rare and irreplaceable books and other texts have been transferred to modern data storage, and all of it is accessible via visitor kiosks stationed throughout the temple. If you prefer physical copies of the original texts, replicas can be obtained in the shrine's gift shop.

## Museum of Vulcan-Andorian Relations

When the Vulcan and Andorian people became aware of each other more than four centuries ago, tensions were high, and confrontations were frequent. This museum traces the evolution of the often-strained interactions between the two worlds, including the hostilities that threatened to erupt into full-scale war during the twenty-second century before both sides agreed to peace and later joined Earth and Tellar Prime in founding the United Federation of Planets. Featured among the displays are the original treaty documents signed by Vulcan and Andorian envoys that brought an end to their conflict, along with the crystal sculptures exchanged between the Vulcan High Command and the Parliament Andoria, each depicting the *kril'es*, a symbol of harmony that serves to unite the two peoples in peace.

## Temples of Syrinx

From bastion of subjugation and intolerance to premier tourist destination, all in less than a millennium. Once the home of a particularly cruel cabal of religious zealots who stood in stark opposition to Surak's philosophies, the Temples of Syrinx fell following a revolt as the communities they oppressed rose up to expel the priests. The ruins of the temples have been a magnet for archaeologists and historians for centuries, as the shrines' inner walls contain engraved incantations and other passages of ancient scripture. Lower-level catacombs are home to the crypts that house the remains of those few priests who escaped public execution. Visitors are free to wander the ruins, and knowledgeable guides are on hand to answer all your questions.

## ▶ Orbital Skydiving

During the earliest days of Vulcan spaceflight, ships fell through the atmosphere and parachuted to a landing in the desert, south of the original spaceport complex. Daring visitors can re-create aspects of that adventure, with no spacecraft required! An observation platform suspended in geosynchronous orbit forty kilometers above Vulcana Regar is your starting point as you freefall from the stratosphere. For beginners, computer-assisted maneuvering thrusters guide you to the landing field and ensure your parachutes are deployed in a safe manner, whereas experienced jumpers can control the entire descent. Just be sure to watch that first step!

## T'Jerel Gallery

A relatively small yet elegant exhibit that highlights the wondrous stone pottery and ceramic creations of T'Jerel, one of Vulcan's most renowned artists of the past several centuries. The gallery itself is too small to house all of her works, so curators reconfigure and rotate the exhibits every few months. Smaller exhibits travel around the planet all year, and there's also a permanent display at the Smithsonian Institution on Earth.

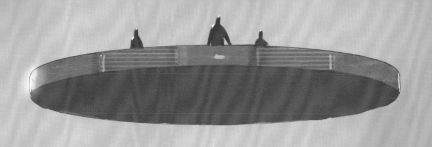

### ▲ Vanik Tower

Space exploration has long been a key component of Vulcan's technological and societal advancement. Among the planet's celebrated explorers is Vanik, who spent more than a century pushing the boundaries of exploration and knowledge. His record of thirty-seven first contacts with new sentient beings remains unmatched, and his tactical prowess was instrumental to the success of the coalition between Vulcans, humans, and Andorians during the Romulan War in the twenty-second century. There are several tributes to Vanik here in the city he called home, but the Tower is by far the most impressive. Originally constructed hundreds of years ago, this ancient temple was renovated in the early twenty-third century and rededicated as a lasting monument. Carved from the top of an immense rock formation near Vulcana Regar's southern boundary, the stone tower features a spiral staircase at its center. The tower's peak is the highest point of natural elevation in the region, offering an unparalleled view of the entire city, including the spaceport complex and points beyond.

## World's Largest Working *Kal-toh* Game

This 50-meter representation of the classic Vulcan strategy game is a favorite for children of all ages along with those adults who are still kids at heart. In an effort to turn the disjointed jumble of playing rods, called *t'an*, into a more ordered form such as a sphere, players use antigravity units to manipulate the individual pieces, which weigh in excess of one thousand kilograms. The game is a popular attraction for tourists and a favorite challenge for experienced *kal-toh* competitors.

## SHOPPING AND ENTERTAINMENT

As you might expect, Vulcana Regar's mercantile center tends to favor the local working-class residents. You'll still find upscale shops, clubs, and other entertainment venues, but the city's true charm is to be found in the hundreds of independently owned boutiques, galleries, restaurants, cafes, and other establishments. There's a nice cosmopolitan flair throughout the city, where local merchants and outworlders have banded together to create an eclectic visitor experience.

### ▶ Desert Racing

A throwback to the time when motorized overland conveyances were popular for individual travelers as well as for moving consumer goods between cities, the Vulcana Regar 1000 attracts drivers of multiwheeled vehicles who are ready to take on the challenge of the race's grueling 1,000-kilometer trek across some of the planet's most unforgiving terrain. The race acquired added notoriety in 2381 when famed Starfleet captain Jean-Luc Picard set a new record for completing the punishing course in just under twenty-seven hours, using nothing more than an unmodified Starfleet all-terrain ground vehicle. Visitors interested in taking on the course themselves can do so as part of a tour group or individually using chartered ATGVs. Additional packages that include overnight camping are also available.

### J'vralek Street Market

In this outdoor shopping center covering seven blocks adjacent to the spaceport's west end, retailers carry a number of avant-garde brands, including prominent Vulcan labels as well as those from worlds as wide-ranging as Risa, Argelius, Deneb IV, and, of course, Ferenginar. Street vendors offer a broad assortment of local and outworlder delicacies, and there are several prime holophotography opportunities with simulations of all manner of local and interplanetary celebrities, government leaders, and fictional characters past and present.

### ◀ Port 47 Imports

You'll not find a single "Made on Vulcan" label here! This popular chain of department stores specializes in goods brought in from dozens of planets. Most of the prominent Federation member worlds and colonies are represented, as well as nonaligned neighbors such as Dolysia, Cantrel V, and Arcturus. Vanilla extract from Tellar Prime? They've got it. Rugs and tapestries from Eminiar? This is the place. Tholian silk? You're covered.

## 🍽 DINING AND NIGHTLIFE

Whatever preconceptions you may harbor about the Vulcan people being quiet and aloof will definitely be challenged when you venture into Vulcana Regar after the sun sets. The nightclub scene here is diverse and lively. There's something for everyone, from traditional restaurants favored by locals to high-end trendsetting establishments catering to well-traveled outworlders.

### Launch Complex Bistro

A relic from Vulcan's early spaceflight program serves as the edifice for this theme restaurant. The gantry tower that once stood alongside rockets launched into orbit offers panoramic views of the nearby spaceport and the rest of the city, while diners enjoy a diverse cuisine representing dozens of Federation worlds. That said, Vulcan fare dominates the menu, and it's here that you'll find the region's best *mia-zed* vegetable pie. A full bar and coffee shop rounds out the presentation, along with a bakery that creates a delicious *favinit* bread pudding. Did we mention you can get the desserts to go?

### Shaukaush

If you're looking for subtlety, this is most definitely not the place for you. Founded by a Risian entrepreneur in the mid-twenty-third century, this after-hours nightclub is strictly for those who want a bit of that famous resort planet's ambience and flair. Only the drinks from the club's well stocked bar have any chance of cooling things down, because everything else is hot. The music is hot, the dancing is hotter, and the dancers—dozens of them crossing numerous genders and species—will all but set the place on fire. The party's even more intense on Friday when the club brings in live music to drive the temperature even higher.

# DID YOU KNOW?
## DON'T EAT WITH YOUR FINGERS!

Picture this common scenario: You're an outworlder tourist, you order a meal at a restaurant or outdoor cafe, and you dig in. Even if you've decided on something as innocuous as a hot dog, you—like many patrons before you—quickly find yourself on the unfortunate end of a withering stare from the local proprietor (who may or may not be Vulcan). What could you possibly have done?

Believe it or not, it's what you're doing with your hands. Vulcans simply do not touch their food with their hands. They consider such behavior to be an unwelcome connection to their far less civilized ancestors, from whom Vulcans have been trying to distance themselves for millennia. No matter what Vulcans are eating, they always employ utensils. This practice means little by itself, and may seem silly from the viewpoint of an outsider, but it is one more small measure of self-discipline Vulcans practice as part of their unending pursuit of logic and emotional control. While this likely isn't a tough transition for most non-Vulcans (at least, those of you who possess appendages), it's definitely something to keep in mind when sampling the local cuisine.

### ▶ Vic's Lounge

What began as a simple holosuite program has gone mainstream and interstellar. Derived from an amalgam of mid-twentieth-century Earth singer/performers, Vic Fontaine is the holographic proprietor of this throwback to ancient entertainment forms, which provides a host of musical selections including jazz and cabaret. While the lounge and its accompanying bar and restaurant maintains the old Earth illusion, another section of the club offers more modern music and dancing selections.

# 🛏 LODGING

You can count on one hand the number of resorts you'll find in Vulcana Regar, though fine hotels and smaller, less lavish accommodations are everywhere. Then there are the purely functional quarters catering to the large number of people just passing through, particularly in and around the spaceport district. A few upscale establishments can be found, too, but they're almost always packed with business travelers and other affluent visitors who don't mind paying top dollar. You should definitely do your homework before booking an extended stay here.

## Tvi'sochya

If tranquility is your goal, this small, unassuming inn might be to your liking. A preferred destination for seasoned travelers, this modestly sized inn of fewer than one hundred suites sits well away from the city and the spaceport. A towering stone wall, which in ancient times offered protection against the sand storms that were known to ravage the area, now insulates guests and staff from the area hubbub while weather-modification satellites keep the storms at bay. The grounds include an immaculately tended garden sprinkled with waterfalls and natural pools that beckon to swimmers.

## The Lazy Le-matya

While it won't make many "best of" lists, this functional if not luxurious water-front hotel serves its purpose well enough. Formerly owned by a local family, the hotel was purchased and renamed a century ago by a Ferengi business exec looking to capitalize on the increased trade between Ferenginar and Vulcan. Though it lacks extravagance, the service is first rate and the food at the attached restaurant, the Starving Sehlat, is a favorite of local freight haulers and port workers.

# VULCAN'S FORGE

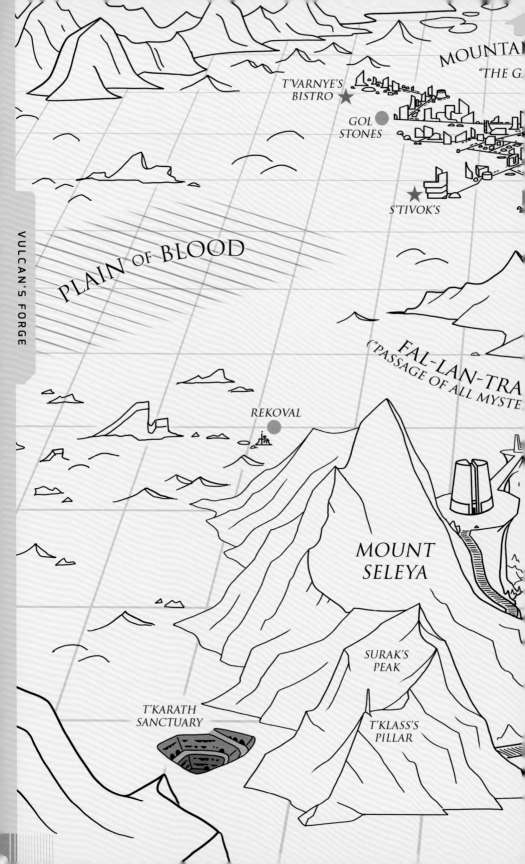

MOUNTA

"THE G

T'VARNYE'S
BISTRO ★

GOL
STONES ●

S'TIVOK'S ★

PLAIN OF BLOOD

FAL-LAN-TRA
("PASSAGE OF ALL MYSTE

REKOVAL ●

MOUNT
SELEYA

SURAK'S
PEAK

T'KARATH
SANCTUARY

T'KLASS'S
PILLAR

OL

GIIDAS
HOTEL

YAUN
MING
CADE

SANDCASTLE
HOTEL

KOLINAHRU
MONASTERY

SHOPPING &
ENTERTAINMENT

DINING &
NIGHTLIFE

LODGING

MARKAN
TE'KORKEL

VULCAN'S FORGE

L-LANGON
MOUNTAINS

# CALL ME A BELIEVER

(First published in the 2286 Edition)

Well, it took me long enough, but so help me, I think I'm actually beginning to like this place.

It took some doing, you understand. First of all, there's the giant contradiction that is Vulcan's Forge. Despite Vulcan's advanced technology and contributions to interstellar knowledge and all of that, the Forge exists as though trapped in amber. Here you'll find the essence of the Vulcan people. Students and masters live and study here as they have for millennia, handing down knowledge and traditions across generations, while seemingly unmoved by the passage of time. It's something to behold, let me tell you.

You'd think I would've picked up on that during my previous visits, but I guess I just didn't appreciate any of it. This time around, though, I've had more of a chance to take it all in. Another thing I never truly realized was just how spiritual these people can be. You wouldn't think that sort of thing would fit with a society that prides itself on logic and reason, and that's before we get into philosophical discussions about science or faith. However, despite all their talk about Vulcans suppressing their emotions, those feelings are an integral part of their personalities, particularly with respect to love and friendship. That much became obvious when Spock gave me his *katra*. Spock's always been a private person and, at first, sifting through his consciousness felt like a tremendous violation. Then I realized that he must have trusted me on a level even deeper than the friendship we'd enjoyed over so many years together by asking me to safeguard something like that.

It's a long story, but Spock's *katra* is back where it belongs, and he's on the road to being back to his old self. As for me, I think I understand him just a little better now. More important, I have a greater appreciation for all Vulcans. You might even say I'm something of a convert, at least when it comes to some aspects of "Vulcan mysticism." If you're curious about such things, then Vulcan's Forge is the destination for you. Sure, it's damned hot, but if you can get past that, there's no better place on the planet to explore the heritage of this unique culture.

Just don't tell Spock I said so.

—Dr. Leonard McCoy

**THE LEAST WELCOMING REGION ON THE PLANET**, "the Forge" still manages to attract a remarkable and growing number of tourists each year. For many, this is the one place that symbolizes everything that is known about Vulcan and its people. An expanse of sprawling desert beyond the L-langon Mountains northeast of ShiKahr, the Forge, along with its most prominent terrain feature, Mount Seleya, has been a prominent location throughout numerous key points in Vulcan history. It is here that young Vulcan children undergo their first tests of maturity, and it is also where those seeking a new life directed by logic travel in order to purge them-selves of their emotions. Desert dominates this region, along with mountains and canyons, and the entire area teems with wildlife. Smaller settlements, monasteries, and other historical sites are situated around the Forge's perimeter, though a few key points of interest are to be found within the expansive interior.

##  GETTING AROUND

We hope you like walking, as that's the primary mode of transportation here, at least in and around those villages and other sites that call the Forge home. Accommodations are available for everyone seeking to venture to some of the outlying historical sites and other points of interest, even those species without appendages or physical forms.

## ◉ SIGHTS AND ACTIVITIES

Most visitors are attracted to the Forge and its surrounding historical sites, of which there are many. Indeed, you could spend an entire vacation just exploring Mount Seleya along the region's southern border. The daytime heat here can be especially harsh, so plan your excursions to take advantage of the numerous interior and subterranean points of interest

### Aerial Tours

The best way to take in the Forge and its numerous landmarks is from the air, using either skiffs piloted by remote control or powered wingflight suits. Either way, knowledgeable guides will direct you up and over this storied region. These tours are best experienced in early morning or dusk, when you can bask in the full glory of a magnificent 40 Eridani sunrise or sunset.

### Hiking and Climbing

The Forge is the apex of hiking on Vulcan. The difficult terrain coupled with unrelenting heat will challenge you like nowhere else on the planet. Trace the same steps taken by Surak as experienced guides lead you over trails walked by this most revered of Vulcans along with many other notable historical figures. If rock climbing is your sport, you'll find challenges in abundance here as well, with seasoned climbing instructors ready to accommodate all skill levels.

### ▶ The Gateway

Not really a geological formation, the Gateway is an area at the Forge's northern end that serves as an entry point into the harsh desert region. Volcanic activity is constant here, as evidenced by the lava pools and steam vents you will encounter as you traverse the winding, mazelike paths through the plains and toward the Mountains of Gol. Due to the extensive lava flows, visitors are forbidden from venturing through the Gateway without guides, although Horta, Excalbians, and similar life forms who thrive in such environments can apply for waivers.

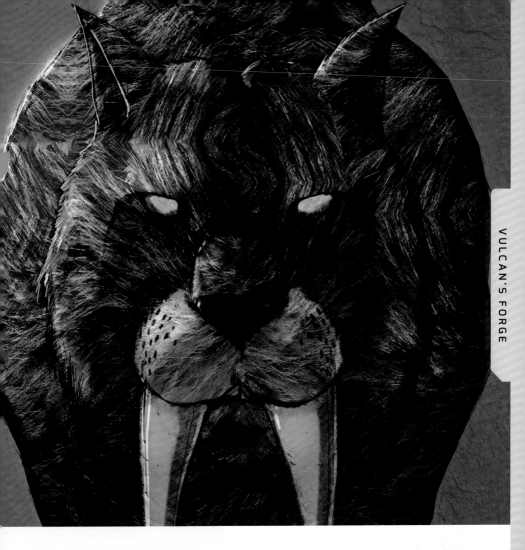

# DID YOU KNOW?
## DON'T PET THE *SEHLATS*.

Though Vulcans have long abstained from the use of animals to assist in laborious tasks, they continue to keep certain quadrupedal life forms as household pets. One of the more popular animals falling into this category is the *sehlat*. Similar to the Ursidae (bear) family of mammals from Earth and the *mIl'oD* found on the Klingon home world, *sehlats* roam many of the planet's mountainous regions and high deserts and are found in abundance here in the Forge.

While untamed specimens can grow quite large and aggressive, the domesticated breeds are usually much smaller. Even then, they require constant training in order to tame their violent tendencies—domesticated *sehlats* can still revert to their feral state if sufficiently alarmed or if they feel threatened. For this reason, those who are not members of a domesticated *sehlat's* family are discouraged from trying to pet or otherwise approach the animal and certainly should not do so without the consent of its master.

## Kolinahru Monastery

One of several religious sites in and around the Forge, this shrine has been home to Adepts and other High Masters for thousands of years. In ancient times, the Kolinahru were considered the foremost practitioners of "dark mental arts," and they used their unequaled influence to terrorize and oppress the surrounding populace through mass mind control, submitting their helpless victims to acts of wanton barbarism. Legends of their cruelty persist to this day. The Kolinahru eventually moved away from such savagery, committing their order to the path of peace. Many of the monastery's texts and artifacts date back generations before the Age of Antiquity, chronicling the evolution of this powerful religious sect.

## *Fal-lan-tral* and the Hall of Ancient Thought

Tucked into the foothills to the north of Mount Seleya and known for generations as the "Passage of All Mysteries," the centuries-old *Fal-lan-tral* path was constructed using blocks of red desert sandstone. The trail leads from the Forge and into the mountain's base, where visitors will find the Hall of Ancient Thought. This revered sanctuary is a labyrinth of mazes, rooms and anterooms, narrow passageways, and tunnels that isolate and protect thousands of *vre'katra*, or crystal vessels, each containing the *katra* of a deceased Vulcan. Access to this hallowed chamber is limited to family members of the departed and rare escorted tours for VIPs. Other rooms within the Hall also house smaller collections of *vre'katra*, and these can be viewed under supervision of a tour guide.

## ▶ Mount Seleya

Located some fifty kilometers from the Forge's southern boundary, Mount Seleya is the region's most prominent geological feature as well as its most sacred site. Indeed, the mountain is a cherished place of worship for many Vulcans who journey here from across the planet. According to legend, it is here that Surak conceived and refined the philosophies of logic over emotion as well as *Kol-Ut-Shan*, or "Infinite Diversity in Infinite Combinations." Clerics, students, and other guides living on or near the mountain are always on hand to regale visitors with the history and stories surrounding the site. A winding stone staircase leads up to an amphitheater near the mountain's top, which plays host to numerous ceremonies throughout the year. Many of these rituals are closed to the public, so don't be surprised if your guide omits this area from your tour.

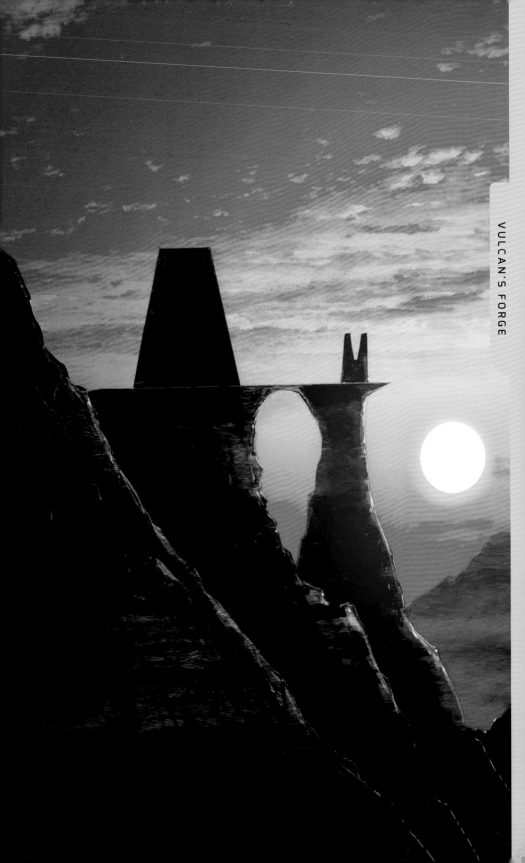

### Surak's Peak

Located near the summit of Mount Seleya, Vulcans consider the peak a holy place as well as a historical site, and great care is taken to preserve the environment. Many Vulcans, particularly *kolinahr* students, travel here to meditate. Guardians of the site conduct guided tours of the peak, and an amphitheater hosts costumed performers who reenact many of the venerated philosopher's most notable speeches.

### ◀ T'Klass's Pillar

This spire of brilliant-red volcanic rock juts nearly five dozen meters upward from the sun-baked soil of Surak's Peak. Some legends describe the pillar as originally being the tip of a massive weapon wielded by Shariel, the god of death, when he took up arms to battle other ancient gods in defense of Sha Ka Ree, the fabled planet from Vulcan mythology where all life was believed to have originated. Scale replicas of the pillar are available in most gift shops.

### Plain of Blood

One of the many battlefields peppering the planet's scorched landscape, the Plain of Blood is testament to the brutal past from which the Vulcan people emerged to become one of the quadrant's preeminent civilizations. According to legends dating back to that distant, violent era, Surak is said to have crossed the Plain when the sands ran green with rivers of blood spilled in the heat of combat, only to cool the scene of carnage with the soothing shroud of logic. Tours of the site depart on the hour from the Mount Seleya visitors' center, and holographic re-creations of the battle can be viewed in the center's amphitheater.

## ▼ T'Karath Sanctuary

This ancient subterranean religious site is situated south of Mount Seleya near the Forge's southern border. Dozens of rooms contain artifacts dating back thousands of years, and curators are on hand to discuss each of the items and their relevance to Vulcan history. When the sanctuary was used as a refuge by Syrrannite rebels in the twenty-second century, the Vulcan High Command ordered it destroyed by aerial bombing. Only the structure's deepest subterranean levels were spared in the attack, though the sanctuary has since been restored to its original condition. The sanctuary's most notable piece is the Kir'Shara, a pyramid-shaped vessel containing Surak's original writings. Believed lost for hundreds of years, the artifact was found in the mid-twenty-second century deep beneath the sanctuary. Its discovery and the revelation of its contents brought about sweeping changes to Vulcan society and a renewed commitment to Surak's philosophies and teachings. Even now, centuries after its discovery, the beliefs it safeguards continue to intrigue and inspire the Vulcan people.

# 🛍 SHOPPING AND ENTERTAINMENT

Despite the overall reserved atmosphere of the Forge's visitor-trafficked areas, you'll still find an assortment of retail shops and tourist-friendly things to do. Most of these establishments are located near the "the Gateway," away from Mount Seleya and the other historical or sacred sites. Several of the locals have managed to find a way to remain respectful of the area's history and legacy while still appealing to outworlders and other visitors who wish to take away a piece of this unique region.

## Gol Stones

This purveyor of rare and antique jewelry and precious metals has something for every occasion and budget. Many of the stones are mined from the nearby mountains and other sites, though there is also a healthy selection of off-world gems. Get your own replica *kolinahr* necklace or *Kol-Ut-Shan* pendant for that special someone back home.

## Rekoval

This modest shop at the base of Mount Seleya trades in replicas of ancient texts, statues of notable Vulcans carved from volcanic rock, and artwork and handcrafted clothing items. The building's glass ceiling affords a spectacular view straight up the side of the mountain to its summit. The shop also features its own tea garden, for which the proprietor grows his own spice plants in order to serve the best *soltar* tea this side of the Forge.

## Mavaun Gaming Arcade

Escape the daytime heat with this state-of-the-art gaming arcade that incorporates full restaurant and bar service and features the hottest titles as well as classic games dating back centuries. Dozens of rooms in this multi-level club, located in the small retail district at the Forge's northern boundary, evoke themes from different worlds. Everything from Ferengi gambling to Wadi interactive holoadventures to twentieth-century-Earth 2D gaming is here. Skill games spit out vouchers redeemable for all manner of "prizes" and other curios, most of which you can find far more cheaply in one of the nearby souvenir shops.

## 🍽 DINING AND NIGHTLIFE

Nightclubs are few and far between here, though there's no shortage of dining options for all dietary considerations. Though Vulcan cuisine naturally is the main attraction, you'll still find a number of restaurants and cafes providing for outworlder tastes. Don't be afraid to sample, though, as a good number of the local eateries grow their own ingredients and make everything fresh daily.

###  S'Tivok's

Here you'll be greeted by the traditionally garbed staff of one of Vulcan's oldest and most celebrated chefs, S'Tivok, who specializes in *t'coraca*, a spicy stew consisting of seventeen different vegetables and half as many seasoning herbs, all of which are grown on the premises. Indeed, the restaurant's interior is an actual garden, which also provides the *soltar* and *n'gaan* plants used to extract ingredients for the various spiced teas. Be sure to try the *kreyla* bread that's baked daily. You'll never again settle for a replicator's recipe.

### T'Varnye's Bistro

Like several other restaurants situated in the tourist-friendly areas lining the Forge's periphery, this diner caters largely to outworlders. Still, the diverse menu attracts many locals and keeps the small, dedicated staff busy night and day. Regulars come for T'Varnye's award-winning *pri tarmeeli*, a spicy vegetable curry that's not for the faint of heart or weak of stomach. Some of the more daring patrons order theirs with extra *c'torr*, a spicy concoction that has earned the nickname *zul*, which translates to "lava." Don't worry; they have milk on the menu, too.

# 🛏️ LODGING

Though there are plenty of hotels and other lodging options in and around the Forge, you won't find the same level of all-inclusive or deluxe accommodations that are common in the larger cities. "Modest" is the operative word here, so if you're looking for a luxury destination from which to launch your Vulcan's Forge adventure, you're better off in ShiKahr or Vulcana Regar. Still, a few of the larger, high-end hotel chains have established footprints here in recent years, and others are giving serious thought to getting in on the action.

### Giidas Hotel

One of the area's more eccentric structures, this hotel is housed within a giant sculpture depicting a quartet of guardian warriors from the Age of Antiquity. Legends tell of groups of such soldiers patrolling the Forge thousands of years ago, always ready to defend against invaders. Originally carved from volcanic rock, the statue was hollowed out and its interior retro-fitted in the late twenty-second century based on the designs of a Vulcan archi-tect. The hotel offers eighteen rooms, though don't expect any sort of view, as the statue's exterior has been preserved in its original state.

### Markan-Te'korkel

In Federation Standard, "the floating palace," more commonly known as the planet's first antigravity hotel, provides an unparalleled view of Mount Seleya and points west. Forty-eight rooms provide guests with an ever-changing view as the entire cylindrical struc-ture rotates in place, completing one clockwise revolution every ten minutes. Guests arrive and depart via trans-porter, as antigravity field generators suspend this wondrous feat of modern engineering fifty meters above the ground. Be sure to spend an afternoon on the rooftop pool, which features a water slide that drops you six levels through the center of the hotel to the crystal clear transparasteel pool that is the structure's underside.

### Sandcastle Hotel

This long-abandoned military fort, carved from sandstone, stood in near ruin until a group of Vulcan historians undertook a restoration effort four centuries ago. Following the comple-tion of the project, an entrepreneur relocating from Risa floated the idea of converting the fort into a hotel while allowing it to retain as much of its original structure as feasible. A large pool and attending canals are the hotel's most inviting external features, allowing guests to relax and rejuvenate while under the care of the attentive staff. Be aware that the hotel operates as if you were vacationing on Risa, complete with all the "permis-siveness" one might expect, so this probably isn't the best place to bring the kids. Yes, *horga'hns* are available for purchase. Use only as directed.

# SURVIVING VULCAN'S FORGE

It's true that the Forge is an inhospitable environment that tests even the strongest and most determined individuals. While tours for outworlders are undertaken with extreme care, and the safety of visitors is of paramount concern, the simple truth is that the Forge is not for everyone, and those electing to venture into the region assume a certain level of personal risk. Here are some tips for staying safe:

- **It's hot.** "Vulcan hot," as many visitors say. Dress appropriately, drink lots of water or whatever fluids or other nutrients sustain your particular physical form, and take care not to overexert yourself.

- **Always be aware of your surroundings.** Yes, the Forge is very beautiful, but it's also just as hazardous. Nothing compares to viewing the Vulcan night sky away from city lights, but just remember that the region's harsh terrain can itself be an enemy. Ravines, crevasses, and cliffs are a danger after dark, so watch where you step, and if you take advantage of an overnight stay as part of your tour package, then pay attention to where you set up your campsite.

- **Don't get lost.** The Forge is big, and there aren't a lot of signs or inhabited places to ask for directions. Stay with your tour group; your guides know where they're going. If you're one of those adventurous types who've thrown caution to the winds and elected to explore on your own, then use GPS gear. Otherwise, safety wardens from the Bureau of Visitor Services might have to send out search parties to find you.

- **Don't get eaten.** Great care is taken to preserve the planet's expansive undeveloped areas and limit the introduction of anything that might damage these fragile ecosystems. *Le-matyas* and other indigenous wildlife subsist on smaller, slower life forms that are native to the region, and the introduction of exotic foodstuffs (e.g. you) may disrupt their diets and have unforeseen effects on the food chain.

# ACKNOWLEDGMENTS

Thanks very much to John Van Citters and Marian Cordry at CBS Consumer Products and Chris Prince at Insight Editions for inviting me to write this book. This was my first time working with Chris and Insight, and it's been a fabulous learning experience.

Hats off and glasses raised to art director Chrissy Kwasnik, designer Jon Glick, and artists Livio Ramondelli and Peter Markowski. These gifted individuals were called upon to provide fantastic work on short notice, and each of them answered the challenge and came through in magnificent fashion. This book is all the better for their creations and other contributions, and I hope I one day get to thank them in person for a tremendous job done so very well.

Special thanks to Michael Okuda and Doug Drexler, graphic artists of the first order. Mike and Doug have been making *Star Trek* look good for a lot of years now, and neither of them batted an eye when I reached out to them for assistance and guidance.

I consulted a number of sources while pulling this book together, including several novels and other *Star Trek* "reference works" published over the years. Even if I only made fleeting mention of something I found in one of these books, websites, or other sources, I tip my hat in appreciation of the authors and dedicated people involved in their publication.

Finally, the last bit of thanks is for my wife and daughters, who make sure I'm fed and loved while working on projects like this, even when I don't sleep that much along the way.

**INSIGHT EDITIONS**
PO Box 3088
San Rafael, CA 94912
www.insighteditions.com

Find us on Facebook:
www.facebook.com/InsightEditions
Follow us on Twitter:
@insighteditions

Published by Insight Editions, San Rafael, California, in
2016. No part of this book may be reproduced in any
form without written permission from the publisher.

Library of Congress Cataloging-in-Publication Data
available.

ISBN: 978-1-60887-520-7

PUBLISHER: Raoul Goff
ACQUISITIONS MANAGER: Robbie Schmidt
ART DIRECTOR: Chrissy Kwasnik
DESIGNER: Jon Glick
EXECUTIVE EDITOR: Vanessa Lopez
SENIOR EDITOR: Chris Prince
PRODUCTION EDITOR: Elaine Ou
ASSOCIATE EDITOR: Katie DeSandro
PRODUCTION MANAGERS: Alix Nicholaeff
and Thomas Chung

Illustrations by Livio Ramondelli and Peter Markowski

## Sources

Bonanno, Margaret Wander. *Star Trek: Strangers from the Sky.* New York: Pocket Books, 1987.

DeCandido, Keith R. A. *Star Trek: Klingon Empire: A Burning House.* New York: Pocket Books, 2008.

Dillard, J.M. *Star Trek V: The Final Frontier.* (A novel based on the screenplay by David Loughery.) New York: Pocket Books, 1989.

———. *Star Trek: The Lost Years.* New York: Pocket Books, 1989.

———. *Star Trek: Recovery.* New York: Pocket Books, 1995.

Duane, Diane. *Star Trek: Spock's World.* New York: Pocket Books, 1988.

Friedman, Michael Jan. *Star Trek: Federation Travel Guide.* New York: Pocket Books, 1997.

Gardner, Mark R, founder. Vulcan Language Institute (VLI). http://home.comcast.net/~markg61/vlif.htm

Hite, Kenneth A., Ross A. Isaacs, Evan Jamieson, Steve Long, Christian Moore, Ree Soesbee, Gareth Michael Skarka, John Snead, and John Wick. *The Way of Kolinahr: The Vulcans.* Last Unicorn Games, 1998.

Interplay Productions. *Star Trek: 25th Anniversary.* Video game. 1991.

Johnson, Shane. *Star Trek: Mr. Scott's Guide to the Enterprise.* New York: Pocket Books, 1987.

Kagan, Janet. *Star Trek: Uhura's Song.* New York: Pocket Books, 1985.

Martin, Michael A. *Star Trek: Enterprise: The Romular War: Beneath the Raptor's Wing.* New York: Pocket Books, 2010.

McIntyre, Vonda N. *Star Trek: The Entropy Effect.* New York: Pocket Books, 1981.

Poteet, Michael S. "The First Law of Metaphysics" in *Star Trek: Strange New Worlds II.* New York: Pocket Books, 1999.

Shatner, William, with Judith and Garfield Reeves-Stevens. *Star Trek: Avenger.* New York: Pocket Books, 1997.

Ward, Dayton. *Star Trek Vanguard: Open Secrets.* New York: Pocket Books, 2009.

Memory Alpha wiki. http://memory-alpha.org.

Memory Beta wiki. http://memory-beta.wikia.com.